THE MARRIAGE HE MUST KEEP

BY
DANI COLLINS

Published in Great Britain 2016
by Mills & Boon, an imprint of Harlequin (UK) Limited,
Eton House, 18-24 Paradise Road, Richmond, Surrey, TW9 1SR

© 2016 Dani Collins

ISBN: 978-0-263-91580-8

Harlequin (UK) Limited's policy is to use papers that are natural,
renewable and recyclable products and made from wood grown in
sustainable forests. The logging and manufacturing processes conform
to the legal environmental regulations of the country of origin.

Printed and bound in Spain
by CPI, Barcelona

Canadian **Dani Collins** knew in high school that she wanted to write romance for a living. Twenty-five years later, after marrying her high school sweetheart, having two kids with him, working several generic office jobs and submitting countless manuscripts, she got 'The Call'. Her first Modern Romance novel won the Reviewers' Choice Award for Best First in Series from *RT Book Reviews*. She now works in her own office, writing romance.

Books by Dani Collins

Mills & Boon Modern Romance

Seduced into the Greek's World
The Russian's Acquisition
An Heir to Bind Them
A Debt Paid in Passion
More than a Convenient Marriage?
No Longer Forbidden?
Vows of Revenge

Seven Sexy Sins

The Sheikh's Sinful Seduction

The 21st Century Gentleman's Club

The Ultimate Seduction

One Night With Consequences

Proof of Their Sin

Visit the Author Profile page at millsandboon.co.uk for more titles.

This book is dedicated to Diane, one of the first Harlequin Presents fans to reach out to me. I know you look for certain things in our books and I had you in mind when I was forming Octavia. I hope you like her.

I also dedicate this book to an angel
and a warrior and their mothers,
my dearest friends, my kids' Other Mothers.
All of your children will be in my heart forever.

CHAPTER ONE

ANOTHER KNIFING PAIN speared into her lower back, radiating like a spiked belt around her middle and clenching her torso in a merciless fist that stole her breath.

"Please call Alessandro," Octavia Ferrante begged in a pant, knotting her fists in the blanket beneath her as she braced herself for the next contraction. She was starting to fear that something would happen and she would never hear his voice again.

Her husband's cousin Primo Ferrante only sighed. His hold on the curtain dropped with disinterest as he turned away from the window. "I told you. He said he would come if the baby is born alive. Otherwise he's not going to put himself out."

She didn't want to believe it. Primo seemed to draw more enjoyment daily from tormenting her. She no longer trusted him and was sure this was more of his games.

But after this many months of being exiled to London by her husband, she was beginning to believe at least some of what Primo said. He was certainly correct in labeling her soft in the head. She'd let her life spiral beyond her grip. Pregnancy was an odd state, making you feel vulnerable in tiny degrees so you didn't realize how defenseless you were until the need to fight arose and there was nothing to draw on. She had insulated herself here, licking her wounds over Alessandro's rejection, and suddenly she had no resources. No one to help her.

Rebellion had backfired on her in the past so she rarely dissented, but she'd never been *weak*. At one time she'd been confident in herself, at least, if not truly assertive. She'd even felt a certain pride in those first few weeks of her marriage—

Another pain tore through her, making her grit her teeth to hold back a scream.

Alessandro, she silently begged, as a fresh wave of perspiration rose to ice her skin. But she knew all about men who wanted live births of their sons. Maybe Primo was telling the truth about her husband's lack of concern.

Call my mother then, she almost said as another pain gripped her, but her mother was also in Italy and would have even less sympathy. Eight times she'd gone through this. Seven of them fruitless labors. Eight, really, since Octavia was hardly counted as a valid heir.

Female. Only good for one thing. This.

Octavia had lived in fear all her life that she would suffer as her mother had, losing babies before she could deliver them. For good reason, apparently. This was not the idealistic, natural process the books promised. This was torture. The baby was coming a month too early, and the pain was terrifying. Something was wrong. She knew it.

"Where is the ambulance?" she cried as the pain throttled back enough that she could catch her breath and speak. "The clinic said to call one as soon as I went into labor. Did you do it?"

"You're being hysterical. These things take hours. You know that," Primo muttered.

He had said he would, but she would bet her life that he hadn't.

"Give me the phone," she demanded, holding out her hand. Why was he even here? Why wasn't her husband?

Her pains were coming on top of themselves. She had to wrap her arm across her swollen middle, fearful her skin would split under the stress.

"Please, Primo. I'm begging you. Take me to the hospital."

"You're an embarrassment to our family name," he said, sneering at her rumpled, sweaty form and tear-streaked face. "Where is all this pride in duty you once told me you had? Show some dignity."

His cruel words, delivered by a cruel man whom she hated with all her being, still had the power to wound. Because Alessandro had left her to this. Each time Primo verbally flayed her, she felt it as an uncaring swipe from Alessandro, like batting a fly. She had been his toy, perhaps, because he'd seemed so taken with her in those early days, but now she was nothing to him. Utterly forgotten. His indifference was a body blow every time she confronted it.

As anguished and defeated as that made her feel, she wasn't about to give birth on her bed, risking her baby's life and her own. Inching to the edge of the mattress, she braced herself on the night table, begging her knees to hold her. She'd crawl out of this room if she had to. Primo might wish her dead, but she wasn't going quietly.

"Is that blood?" Primo demanded sharply. His hawk-like gaze swooped from her tense face to the spotted blanket and back. His complexion grayed.

As she looked at the small mark, what little body heat remained in her drained from her face and chest and limbs. This was it, then. Like her mother, she was doomed to lose her baby. If she survived, this would happen again and again as she tried to live up to her side of the marital contract. Why, oh, why had she thought going through with an arranged marriage would finally earn her some respect from her father? Why had she let herself begin to care for her husband, hoping to earn his affection?

Why had she opened her heart and taken this unborn infant deep inside it, believing that finally there would be a human on this earth who loved her back?

No one was ever going to love her. She was the only person she could rely on. It was time to face that.

With a sob, she staggered across to where he'd left her phone on the windowsill and snatched it up. Bowing her head against the wall, silently praying, she dialed the number for emergency services and told them to send an ambulance.

Alessandro Ferrante saw his wife was calling and his pulse tripped. He immediately tamped down on the involuntary reaction, ruthlessly regaining control over himself and annoyed that he let her catch him so easily, even when she was on the other side of the continent.

But some measure of surprise was legitimate. She never called him anymore.

Which he was trying not to let bother him.

"Cara," he answered, ears straining for clues as to why she was calling now. It was late in London, even later here in Naples, but apparently they were both still up. Perhaps the baby was kicking. She had said a few times that she had trouble sleeping through that. It had made him feel the distance between them quite keenly...

He ignored the stab of something that might have been regret. The separation was necessary. He wouldn't give in to weak yearnings and wind up putting her in danger. That would be irresponsible.

"Sono io," Primo said into his ear. *It's me.*

Not Octavia then. Disappointment fell through him before he could deflect it. He habitually fought extreme degrees of emotion, never allowing them to rule his actions, but this marriage was becoming so very much *not* a marriage and it was beginning to frustrate him. It had started with such promise. They had had a remarkable compatibility, particularly in bed, but it had disintegrated into something he didn't know what to do with anymore.

Not for the first time, he questioned his decision to leave her in London, but all the facts remained the same: she was pregnant and at risk. Her mother had a history of losing babies. His mother's house in London was in the same city as a world-class specialist clinic, one that had been monitoring her closely. She was also safe from the threats here in Naples. His refusal to bring her home was absolutely the best thing for her and their unborn child.

His wife had taken to avoiding his calls, however. His cousin made all her reports, which was an intrusion Alessandro didn't appreciate. Why was Primo even still at his mother's house? How long did it take to get an apartment painted these days?

"Si?" Alessandro prompted his cousin now, tone sharpening with dismay.

"She's gone into labor," Primo said bluntly.

Alessandro sat up, arteries stinging with an immediate shot of adrenaline, the desk full of work before him forgotten. This was too early. Almost a month before her due date. He had planned to fly out next week. He reached for his tablet, already tapping out a message to his driver and pilot.

"It all happened very quickly or I would have called you sooner," Primo continued. "The ambulance was delayed and—well, there have been complications."

Silence followed.

Alessandro waited.

A knife of dread went through him, impossible to dodge. Primo liked to frame things in as much drama as possible. Sandro had talked to him about it more than once, told him that it only exacerbated situations, but Primo loved to grab and hold attention.

This wasn't the time.

Unless Primo was truly reluctant to deliver bad news.

Alessandro could hear the ticking of the clock that had been in his family for generations—*tick, tick, tick*. Like a bomb. He couldn't breathe. He was paralyzed, completely devoid of feeling and his mind was empty as he held off what he feared would be a repeat of another moment when tragedy unfolded. When tires screeched and—

"Yes?" he prompted, throat raspy and thick.

"They had to take her to the nearest hospital, not the one where she was scheduled to deliver. It's inundated with a bus crash, but they're taking her for surgery right now."

His nerves exploded with a rush of urgency, barely rational.

"Which hospital?" Alessandro demanded, fighting a ferocious grip of emotion that wanted to overstep reason and break down doors and walls and laws of man and nature to reach London. He grappled to stay calm, forcing himself to speak clearly even as his mind and heart raced. "I'm leaving now. I'll be there as soon as I can."

CHAPTER TWO

SCORE ONE FOR state-run hospitals, was Octavia's first clear thought as her muddled brain came back from the anesthetic and worked out that Primo had no access to her son.

While he had followed her ambulance, she had clasped the female paramedic's hand, a kind of desperate fury gripping her. "Primo is not my husband. Not the father. Do not allow him near my baby. Tell the hospital to keep him out of the delivery room. I *will* hold you responsible if something happens."

She still felt irrational for saying it, but she just didn't trust him. Not after the way he'd moved into the mansion as if he owned it and had taken such great pains to make her miserable while he was there.

Despite his premature birth, her son was thankfully doing well. He was being kept in an incubator for observation and the nurse was about to take Octavia to the nursery to feed him.

The staff here was nice, treating her with more warmth and kindness than she'd seen in months. And Alessandro was on his way. He should be here soon, Primo had begrudgingly told her as he'd paced her room.

Because it was a boy? Octavia tried not to feel bitter. Her father would be pleased, she supposed. Oddly, she discovered that she no longer cared what the men in her life expected of her. There was only one male to whom she wanted to answer and that would be on her own terms as his mother.

Still, part of her fluttered with a mixture of excitement and anxiety, knowing she'd finally see Alessandro again. He hadn't been here since Christmas and that had been a very brief few days. They hadn't even shared a bed, let alone the physical loving she'd been craving. Her condition had cut that off months ago.

Primo was telling the truth about one thing, she supposed. Alessandro not only thought she was fat and unattractive, but was taking his pleasure elsewhere.

So she shouldn't be feeling like this: as conflicted as she'd been in the weeks leading up to their wedding, when she'd been tormenting herself with worry over their wedding night. Would he think she was pretty? Would she please him?

With a pang in her heart, she recalled how silly it had been to stress about that side of things. Lovemaking had turned out to be the least of her concerns. Once they got past her virginal inhibitions, she'd adored making love with him, discovering things about herself and the fit of man and woman that astonished her.

But sex—or rather, lack thereof—had become yet one more way Alessandro had been showing her how little she interested him these days. It made her feel needy and pathetic that she ached for his attention, both in bed and out.

She'd learned long ago to roll that lonely emptiness into a wall of aloof indifference, though. She just wished she could feel aloof or indifferent at his impending arrival. But she couldn't.

"Mrs. Ferrante," the nurse, Wendy, greeted her as she brought in the empty wheelchair she'd fetched. "Let's take you to your little man."

Primo made no move to help Octavia and she was grateful, even though her emergency surgery had annihilated her abdominal muscles and the anesthetic still had her feeling nauseous and weak.

He did follow them from the room to the door of the nursery, though, obviously under the impression he could enter with them.

Wendy, bless her, said, "I'm sorry. Parents only in the nursery."

"Octavia," he prompted firmly.

"You'll have to meet Alessandro and show him where we are," she replied innocently.

The hospital wasn't that big. Alessandro was a resourceful man. He'd find her just fine, but Wendy was buzzing them into the nursery with her security card and the bright, warm room washed over Octavia like a hug of welcome. Beyond the windows, beams of morning sunlight broke the gray clouds hovering over London, sending angelic rays onto the rooftops and giving Octavia a lift of hope for the first time in ages.

"He's been calling for you," the heavyset nurse inside the nursery said. Her name tag read Hannah. "I'll fetch Miss Kelly while you're in here to keep an eye on this one," she said to Wendy, nodding at the only other baby in the room.

"The calm after the storm," Octavia said as she gingerly moved herself into one of the padded rocking chairs. "The emergency room was a zoo when I arrived last night."

The chaos had been alarming, adding to what was already a frightening situation. Tears of relief stung her eyes as she finally felt as if she could relax and hold the baby she'd been so worried for.

"I heard," Wendy responded as she gathered up the fussing baby from the incubator labeled Ferrante and loosely wrapped his diapered form in a blanket. "That's why Dr. Reynolds isn't in to see you yet. She had these two deliveries back-to-back, then they asked her to assist with that tourist bus crash that came in right before you two. She was here very late. Everyone was on their toes for hours. One of you was actually sewn up by our cosmetic surgeon so Dr. Reynolds could run to the other. Yes, we hear you, Mr. February," Wendy said as the baby in the other incubator grew more insistent.

Wendy came across to her, but something in the other baby's cry gave Octavia a stab of fretfulness. It was disconcerting, but Wendy distracted her, waiting with her baby, saying, "You'll want to take your arm out of the sleeve of your gown."

Octavia did, feeling immodest as she bared her breast, even though it was only her and the nurse in this very warm room. The baby Wendy offered her was clearly distressed and famished.

Goodness both babies had a pair of lungs. As Wendy placed her son in her arms, his warm weight filled Octavia with a rush of protective emotions. He was wiggly and endearing, very handsome with a shadow of silky black hair showing from beneath his little blue-and-white-striped cap. His eyelashes and eyebrows were so faint they were barely there, his nose a button, his disgruntled expression almost laughable.

But…

A strange chill went through her.

"That's what we've been calling them. Mr. January and Mr. February," Wendy chattered on. "Since they were born barely an hour apart, but in different months. Do you have a name picked out? Let him find your nipple," she prompted.

"I was waiting for my husband to finalize his name,"

Octavia replied in a murmur, but broke off as the baby's arm waved and his little face rooted against the swell of her breast. He was adorable, so cute in his determination. He rather stole her heart in a way, but drawing him to her breast felt wrong.

Oh, dear God, was this what had happened to her mother? She'd finally birthed Octavia, a live baby, and had wanted to meet the basic needs of her daughter, but failed to feel a wash of true, maternal love?

Octavia's world crashed in on itself. She was such a failure. An utter failure. First as a child, then as a wife. Now as a mother. No wonder no one loved her. She was incapable of feeling the emotion herself.

Tears rushed up to cling to her lashes. She blinked hard. One fell onto the scrunched-up face of the infant. She wiped it away, trying to find something in his tiny features that would provoke that feeling she had had during her pregnancy. The one that had told her this baby was connected to her. Indelibly.

But it didn't come.

This was wrong. The boy grew more frantic, his high-pitched cries breaking her heart, but there was nothing of herself in him. Nothing familiar. He looked wrong. Not bad or repulsive or ill or damaged. Just…wrong.

He arched his little back and let out demanding, furious squawks.

"The first time is always awkward," Wendy assured her, reaching to assist. "You're not the first to cry. Just let him—"

"No," Octavia said, asserting herself with more strength than she had realized she possessed, but this was the oddest sensation she'd ever felt. She wanted to help this baby. He was obviously hungry and distraught and so helpless. She wanted to feed him, but the words just came out. "This isn't my baby."

* * *

Alessandro hadn't slept. He'd piloted his private jet himself and sped through a mess of winter weather to arrive in London as quickly as possible. It was exactly the sort of recklessness he would lecture anyone else against, but he was here and that was the result he had sought.

On landing, he picked up the message that his son was born. He was being kept in an incubator as a precaution since he was a few weeks premature, but he was otherwise healthy.

Good news, but Primo had said nothing about Octavia, which Alessandro suspected was deliberate. Couldn't Primo see there was a place for jocular games and this wasn't it? Alessandro loved his cousin, but Primo was compelled to taunt and make power plays at every turn. When would he grow up and quit swiping at him for a decision made by their grandfather?

Stepping onto the curb next to his pensive cousin, Alessandro demanded, "How is she?"

"How am I to know?" Primo dropped his cigarette and stamped it out, then gave Alessandro's security detail a look that was difficult to interpret. Like he viewed the bodyguards as an affectation, making Alessandro bristle.

"She doesn't talk to me," Primo continued. "Didn't tell me she was hemorrhaging. I suppose the surgery went well enough, since she's alive, but it's like she didn't want to make it to the hospital in time. This hospital is a joke, by the way. She put herself and the boy at risk. Honestly, Sandro, I told you I wonder about her mental health and this is a perfect example."

Alive. His heart finally settled into a normal, healthy beat, making him aware of how high his blood pressure had been.

"Women are emotional during pregnancy," he reminded

his cousin, striding into the hospital. "Why do you take these things so personally?" He was such a prima donna, not that Alessandro had ever called him that aloud. He would never hear the end of it, but his cousin's narcissism grated. Things were fraught enough without Primo waving his hands in the air.

But Primo still had his father and the bunch of them were as animated as any Italian family. Sandro was the wet blanket of the clan, consistently reminding everyone that lack of forethought could have dire consequences.

"It's more than that, Sandro," Primo insisted, pacing him. "She says things that don't make sense."

Alessandro schooled himself against making a patronizing remark that at least Octavia didn't constantly border on hysteria, but he had some concerns for her mental state all the same. He'd noticed small inconsistencies in Primo's reports against what Octavia had told him via text and email. Her odd relationship with her parents, so detached, had made an impression on him from the beginning.

Her mother had a tendency toward depression, Alessandro had come to recognize, but he had hoped his wife wasn't prone to it, as well. She'd been bashful in their early weeks of marriage, gradually opening up in a way that had delighted him, but she'd become downright withdrawn in the past months, which worried him.

She had been pregnant, though. He'd watched enough sisters and cousins go through the process to know that every woman behaved differently as she came to terms with the way her body and life was changing. He had told himself that all of this was normal and temporary.

Primo steered him up the stairs then down the hall to an empty room. He should have brought flowers, Alessandro realized belatedly, and was startled by a lurch in his middle as he stared at the unoccupied bed. He had been counting on seeing her.

"She must still be in the nursery," Primo said, stepping into the hall to point toward the end. "They may not let you in. She was being very touchy, didn't want to let me see him. Honestly, Sandro, this animosity she has… We're family. I understand that she's an only child and is jealous of me, that it threatens her that you and I are so close, but I'm only trying to look out for her. *You asked me to.* Will you explain that to her? Again? Please?" He tagged on the last with a testy roll of his eyes.

Alessandro hadn't *asked* his cousin to look after his wife. He had said once that it had been kind of Primo to take Octavia to her doctor appointment. Frankly, he'd hoped Primo's staying at the mansion would help the two of them get past that small discord from the night they'd all met, but it hadn't happened. Sensing the tension, Alessandro had actually suggested Primo find other accommodation when he had been here at Christmas. Primo had assured him the renovations to his apartment were almost finished.

"I'm here to look after her now," Alessandro said, and, since the death threats hadn't been repeated, he added, "She and the baby will come back to Naples with me once she's released. You can focus on work."

"About that, there are things we need to discuss," Primo said with abrupt urgency.

"They'll have to keep," Alessandro said, thinking that Octavia was not the only one who was jealous. Primo couldn't stand being upstaged ever, which was the foundation of his acts of rivalry. Normally, Alessandro would do what he could to keep the peace, but today he had higher priorities. "I would like to meet my son, Primo. Go back to Mother's and get some rest."

He motioned to a nurse as he continued toward the nursery, vaguely aware of Primo falling back, but the focus of his attention was now firmly fixed on Octavia and his child. "Thank you," he said to the nurse after identifying himself and being buzzed into the nursery.

It was a surprisingly noisy place. Babies were crying, a nurse was speaking plaintively, and Octavia's voice, always clear and modulated, never whiny or harsh, said firmly, "I can see he's hungry and I'm telling you I *will* feed him, but with a bottle."

"Octavia?" Alessandro moved forward and the nurse standing in front of her stepped aside, an uneasy look on her face.

The anticipation rising in him skewed to concern. His wife looked…breakable. Wan. As if she was barely holding herself together. Her eyes, dark as the petals of black pansies, were pools of fraught distress. Her luscious mouth, the lips he loved to devour, were pinched in torment. The roundness in her face and bare shoulder took him by surprise. Her weight gain through the pregnancy hadn't been tremendous, but he hadn't seen her often enough to be used to it. It made her seem that much softer. Vulnerable.

And so feminine, still so beautiful and womanly with her hair loose and her face clean of makeup that his libido responded. How? How could he not go five seconds in her presence without experiencing a rush of heat to his groin and a lurch of possessiveness in his gut? It was maddening to have such a primeval reaction and not be able to control it.

For the merest hint of a second, as their gazes locked, he saw a flash of…something. The thing he saw when she woke beside him. The smile that began to glimmer before it reached her lips.

Then it was gone.

She adjusted her hospital gown self-consciously and shifted the baby up to her shoulder, rocking with agitation in the gliding chair, trying anxiously to soothe the baby who sounded positively desolate.

"Alessandro." She kept her lashes lowered.

Not *caro*. Not even Sandro. He tried to recall the last time she'd greeted him in a way that sounded the least bit welcoming or friendly.

When had she last really looked at him? Met his gaze for longer than a millisecond?

But if he had a moment of regret that leaving her in London had impacted their marriage, his sense of duty smothered it. Every decision he made was for the sake of the Ferrante family. He had shunned marrying for love quite deliberately. His wife was an asset, a strength, not a weakness.

Still, her rebuff grated after his difficult journey to reach her.

The nurse gave him a pleading, *I don't know what to do* look, putting him further on edge. He loathed emotional chaos and had been drowning in it since Primo's call. Why the hell wasn't anyone taking things in hand here?

"Is there a problem?" he asked, taking control himself.

"Your wife wants to use a bottle, but you don't want to introduce one this early," the nurse insisted to Octavia. "It causes nipple confusion. He might not take to the breast after."

"You don't want to feed him yourself?" Alessandro was genuinely shocked. He and Octavia hadn't talked about how she would feed the baby and women had a choice about these things, he supposed. He wasn't sure why he took her decision like a slap, but coming on the heels of her cool greeting, he had never felt so summarily rejected in his life.

"Look at him," she said with a tremble in her voice, and showed him the baby.

The infant was red-faced and frantic, abrading Alessandro's nerves with his cries. *Just feed him,* he thought, unable to fathom why she couldn't see that's what the baby wanted.

"And look at that one." She pointed to the incubator on the other side of the room. It was clearly labeled Kelly.

Alessandro looked from the incubator back to his wife. Then to the fussing infant she held. Then to the nurse. Then back to the incubator.

He was not a stupid man, but he didn't understand. And it made him uneasy that he didn't understand. It was too foreign an experience.

"The tags are in order, Mr. Ferrante," Wendy assured him. "We follow very tight protocols. When the head nurse gets back, she'll explain. This is your baby." She pointed to the one that Octavia held.

"Look at that one," Octavia demanded vehemently enough that Alessandro was impelled across to view the other infant inside the dome.

The boy was on his side, naked but for a diaper, limbs moving in slow flails. He looked forsaken, bawling alone in there, catching at Sandro's heart. He had the urge to pick him up and try to soothe him. This boy was literally crying out for human touch, but that would have to come from parents with the last name of Kelly. Obviously.

Nevertheless, he found himself unable to lift his gaze, locking on to the few wisps of black hair that poked from beneath the baby's green-and-white-striped cap. Something in the fine silkiness made Sandro think of the delicate strands at Octavia's temple and the back of her neck, but the tag on this baby's ankle read Kelly.

Exhaustion was catching up to him if he was having delusions. Octavia had been through a lot, he reminded himself, using mammoth effort to scale himself back to cool reason. He had thought Octavia one of the most rational people in his life, but she was only human and possibly still foggy from whatever drugs they might be feeding her.

He looked back at her and for once he held her complete attention, as if she was sending silent brain waves at him, trying to induce him toward something.

"She won't give him to me," Octavia said, husky voice wavering between acute anger and a deep suffering that tugged at a deep place inside him.

"He's not your baby, Mrs. Ferrante," the nurse maintained.

"This is not my son," Octavia returned, red and frazzled as she tried to calm the baby bellyaching on her shoulder.

Alessandro had to use a long mental reach to find his patience, but he was well practiced at maintaining his composure. Snapping and acting on impulse, no matter how tempting, was not the sort of behavior he exhibited, ever. Italian or not, his mother's son or not, his displays of passion were confined to the bedroom.

"Bring me a bottle. I'll feed him," he ordered the nurse. "My wife is obviously having reservations. It's her body, so…"

"That is not—I'll feed *my* baby," Octavia cried, looking up at him in a way that was halfway between forceful and vanquished. Betrayed and misunderstood.

Disappointed.

As stung as he was by her rejection of their son, as shocked as he was to see her throw a tantrum, something moved in him. Uncertainty.

But she had to be wrong. Mix-ups didn't happen. She was holding their baby. Wasn't she?

Her gradual rejection of him the past months crept over

him like a frost. Why didn't she want him anymore? Why wouldn't she accept his child?

Wendy left to prepare a bottle, of course, because when Alessandro spoke, people listened. No one ever jumped like that when Octavia spoke.

And no one had ever managed to look at her quite like that, as if she was something he wanted to scrape off the bottom of his shoe like cold, fetid mud.

Octavia dropped her gaze, unable to meet his eyes. He was far too handsome anyway, shrugging out of his leather aviator jacket so his muscles strained against the clinging knit of the light blue pullover he wore. His stubbled cheeks were the only sign of his long night in the air. The rest of him was crisp gray pants, hair ruffled and starting to curl where it was a little too long on top, and those gray-green eyes that penetrated like a persistent tropical rain.

Everything about him was strength. Level shoulders, steady mouth, composed brow. His face had a perfect bone structure of clean lines, like his maker had used a ruler while drawing his features, leaving sharp angles at his cheekbones and making a straight slope of his nose before finally softening with freehand for his lips.

His sinful lips. She shouldn't be thinking of all the wonderful things that mouth had done to her. Carnal things.

That mouth was pursed in distaste at her unbelievable claim.

Patting the baby she held, Octavia tried desperately to comfort him while seeking comfort herself. Was she crazy? Primo was always quick to ask her that. *Are you on drugs? Have you lost your mind? Do you think like normal people? How could you imagine such a thing?*

Months of those sorts of queries had left her questioning her own sanity. Why was she in London, isolated from all that was familiar, carrying a baby the father seemed to care nothing about? Why wasn't she fighting for a better situation? At the very least, she should have insisted on some sort of contact or acknowledgement from her husband. Why hadn't she demanded that he speak to her firsthand, not second?

Being here in London had been like boarding school, something to be endured. She hadn't been in physical peril, merely unhappy. Her mother had spent her entire life unhappy. Such was the lot of a wife who was a pawn in male ambition. Who would have had any pity for Octavia? Poor little rich girl, whining because she had to live in a mansion with servants and all the shopping she could stand.

Being the tolerant, patient sort, she'd thought her husband would eventually show up and make her feel special again. She had believed in the vision of a warm and loving family, that was the problem, yet here she was being denied even the right to hold her own baby.

Being tolerant and patient and obedient and dutiful were all starting to look like the stupidest things she'd ever done.

Rocking jerkily, she gently bounced the baby she held, mind whirling. That baby over there looked like Alessandro. Couldn't he see it? She'd argued with the nurse until she couldn't stay on her feet any longer or risk dropping the baby she'd been given. The woman had refused to let her have him, but it was obvious to anyone with functioning eyes. Why wasn't her husband backing her up? If he couldn't see it, perhaps she really was cracked.

But his cry, that baby's cry, muted as it was by the incubator, was tearing her up. So was this one's. She felt like the worst person in the world, unable to help him, but she couldn't feed him from her breast. That boy over there was her son. That was the baby her body yearned to nurture. She *knew* it.

Into the din of crying infants and the staccato glide of her chair, the door gave a click and a woman's chattering voice entered.

"—expected to deliver naturally, but the cord— Oh, hello. I heard we were competing for the surgeon's attention last night. I'm Sorcha Kelly." The blonde in the wheelchair was beautiful. Her hair was pulled into a clip and her oval face was clear and pale. She hadn't puffed up the way Octavia had. When her curious gaze lifted to Alessandro's, it made Octavia tense with jealousy.

Bracing herself, Octavia glanced up, certain Alessandro would be noticing and responding to a smile that wasn't exactly an invitation, but what man could resist such fresh-faced beauty?

He offered a polite nod and a distant introduction. "Alessandro Ferrante. My wife, Octavia, and our son, Lorenzo. That is the name we agreed upon, is it not?" he said to Octavia, willing her to accept that much at least.

All she could manage was a tiny nod and a shrug. Yes, she wanted to call her son Lorenzo, but that name didn't match this baby.

Alessandro's dour look stilled the air in her throat, making it impossible for her to say so. Why did he have to look at her with such disdain? She could practically hear him thinking, *Just like Mother*, but she wasn't making a scene on purpose!

She opened her mouth to plead her case, but Sorcha Kelly was holding out her arms for the baby that her nurse had fetched and loosely wrapped. The nurse asked Alessandro to turn his back and he did with a brisk apology, dragging his gaze off the other infant and giving Sorcha the privacy she needed to settle in the rocker with one breast bared.

A lightning streak of anguish burned through Octavia, singeing her heart into a dark, powdered coal as she watched Sorcha close her arms around the baby.

"I've been waiting to meet you, Mr. Kelly." Sorcha's expression was filled with anticipation and sweet joy.

Octavia finally found her voice. "That's—"

"Octavia," Alessandro said, his tone soft yet deadly.

She took a shaken breath, glanced into eyes that might have been shadowed with something more than disparagement. Offense? Injury? It caused a dip and roll in her chest, but anxiety had her quickly shifting her attention back to Sorcha.

The other woman had cocked her head. Her brows pulled together as she smiled crookedly at the overwrought infant she held. The nurse urged Sorcha to put the baby to her breast.

"I don't think—" Sorcha's gaze came up and straight across to the baby Octavia was trying to soothe, rubbing his back and rocking him.

"The bottle, sir," Wendy said, returning to hand something to Alessandro.

Octavia was aware of them in her periphery, but her entire world fuzzed at the edges as she met Sorcha's troubled gaze. The only thing that mattered was that baby Sorcha held. *Her* baby.

Sorcha's gaze clashed with Octavia's, apprehensive and confused. Gently, Octavia lowered the baby she held so Sorcha could see his face.

They were only a few meters apart. It was very easy to see Sorcha's eyes widen in shock, to interpret her expression as the kind of terrified alarm that only a mother whose baby was in peril would wear. As if he was falling out a window.

"How did you—" Sorcha began in a tone of accusation, then quickly bared the ankle of the boy she held, hand shaking as she looked at his tag. Her panicked gaze came back to Octavia's.

"They wouldn't believe me," Octavia said, voice so thin she barely heard it herself.

"Believe what?" Sorcha's nurse asked, while the nurse who'd been torturing Octavia tried to stammer out statements of protocol again.

"My wife is confused," Alessandro said and bent to reach for the baby Octavia held.

She tightened her arms around him, refusing to give up the infant.

At the same time, Sorcha blurted, "Don't. Don't touch him." She struggled to her feet and hitched her gown over her breast, then came across to Octavia.

"No one would believe me," Octavia told her again, motherly instincts rising hard as her own baby approached. Her eyes stung and her heart hurt. "I wanted to feed him, but he needs his own mama and they wouldn't give me mine…"

Her words garbled into a choke of emotion as she and Sorcha clumsily exchanged infants.

"I believe you," Sorcha said with a wobbling smile, kissing her baby's cheek as she took him, drawing him close against her chest with tender care. "Of course we know our own babies."

Octavia nodded in gratitude, thinking she would be Sorcha's slave forever, she was so thankful. *This* was Lorenzo. He smelled right and fit her arms and his skin was so soft and right against her lips. His little body was startlingly strong despite being racked by crying for a good twenty minutes. Oh, he had his father's ferociously determined face, looking as though he would get exactly what he wanted no matter what he had to do.

He latched perfectly, quieting in synchronicity with his nursery mate.

Octavia sighed with relief and exchanged a teary smile with Sorcha, then became aware of the thick silence. The nurses were staring at them, mouths agape.

Alessandro was thunderstruck.

CHAPTER THREE

"WHAT ARE YOU *DOING*?" Alessandro asked Octavia, feeling as though he'd hit black ice and was skidding toward an abyss. Never in his life had he seen anything like what had just happened.

"Can't you see they mixed them up? Look at him." She gently adjusted the blanket with a trembling hand, ensuring the baby was kept warm, but allowing Alessandro to see the boy's face.

Now she showed an inclination toward love, but to whose child?

Was he as unhinged as she was that he thought he saw a resemblance in that baby's features to the various scrunched faces he'd seen on his infant nephews? He'd always thought all babies looked alike at that age, but…

Octavia's frenetic pace on the rocker had slowed. She looked far more at peace, much more like the composed woman he knew her to be. It was finally quiet enough in here that he could think, but he simply couldn't wrap his brain around what had just happened. Had she somehow conspired with that other woman to switch his own son with a stranger's? Or had the hospital genuinely mixed up something as important as two babies?

"It's impossible," one of the nurses said, echoing his thoughts. "We have very strict protocols. They couldn't have been switched. You shouldn't be doing this. You both have it wrong."

"*You* have it wrong," the other mother, Sorcha, said. "Test them. You'll see we're right."

Alessandro was trying to afford that woman some privacy, but he could see Octavia staring over at Sorcha with solidarity in her expression that was so fervent, it gave him pause. She had welcomed this second infant so tenderly. What if she was right?

"This is beyond anything I've ever encountered," he pronounced, cutting into a discussion between the nurses about how completely impossible a mix-up could be. "Run the tests. Immediately."

"Of course, sir, but the doctor will have to order it. I'll phone straightaway," she assured him.

"Didn't *I* suggest tests?" Sorcha murmured dryly to Octavia.

"Women's voices are so high only dogs hear them," Octavia retorted, revealing the sense of humor she'd kept hidden from Alessandro since the first weeks after their honeymoon.

As soon as she realized he'd heard her, she sobered, expression ironing into the passive mask he was beginning to realize was a special look she adopted just for him. It shot an arrow of discomfort into his chest, lodging there and vibrating, but he dismissed it, determined to get to the bottom of the babies' identities. That was paramount.

Her expression softened as she looked down at the baby. Lorenzo, if that was indeed their son, had fallen asleep. Carefully pulling him off her nipple and adjusting her gown so her breast was covered, Octavia brought him to her shoulder and rubbed his back, looking so natural and content, eyes closed and the most loving of smiles on her lips, that Alessandro had to swallow a lump of emotion.

"Maybe you should stick with the bottle, Mrs. Ferrante, until things are made clear," her nurse said.

"Things are very clear," Octavia said, lifting heavy eyelids, but sounding surprisingly fierce. "This baby is mine and I'm not letting him out of my arms until you've all accepted that."

Her gaze shifted to slam into Alessandro's with banked animosity, including him in her statement. More than just a mother bear, she was a jungle cat capable of clawing him to pieces and eating him alive if he crossed her.

Even more unexpectedly, her revelation of such pure aggressive emotion turned him on.

Lorenzo was surprisingly heavy. Octavia wished they could all go back to her room where she could lie down with her baby and rest.

She wanted to ask Alessandro if he wanted to hold his son. He should have demanded the opportunity by now, she thought, but he was too busy conducting a razor-sharp interview of the nurses on their newborn-tagging procedures.

Even she had to admit, given the precautions in place, the chance of a mix-up was very low. Still, it had happened. She couldn't prove it, but she knew it.

A rush of tears threatened to overwhelm her as she faced the challenge of substantiating what was merely an instinct.

Fortunately Dr. Reynolds arrived and involved the hospital administration immediately. "DNA tests take time. We'll do one, of course, but we'll do a quick blood test right now," Dr. Reynolds said. "It won't be conclusive, but it could certainly determine if a baby is *not* with the right pair of parents."

"Excellent." Alessandro began rolling up his sleeve, so used to having people jump the minute a decision was made, he expected nothing less than to have a needle plunged into his arm right this second. "I believe I'm a B, but test to confirm it."

It all took time, however. A technician from the lab had to come up. The hospital administrator wanted to witness and sign off on the labeling, and interview both mothers. The night staff was being called in for questioning. Security was reviewing records of comings and goings to see if there'd been interference.

At least Octavia had an ally in Sorcha. Yes, Alessandro was determined to get to the bottom of things, but Octavia couldn't help feeling that he was blaming her. She'd seen that hard-faced look before, usually when his mother was around, saying outrageous things and demanding to be the center of attention.

When he came across to her, she almost flinched from his hand on her shoulder.

He noticed, shock flickering in his expression before he gentled his touch into a soothing caress.

"I'm going with the administrator to speak with their head of security." He still sounded gruff and looked terrible. Tired and stressed, but that air of grit was oddly reassuring as he added, "I want to see for myself whether their procedures were followed. This is unacceptable. There shouldn't be any doubt."

His gaze dropped to the sleeping baby and a flash of torture cut across his expression before he suppressed it. He might not be ready to believe her—he was too much a man of facts and process to follow someone's gut instinct, even his wife's—but he wasn't discounting her, either.

Before she could react, he cupped the side of her face and leaned in. His mouth covered hers in a brief, damp openmouthed kiss that shot a jolt of excitement through her, stopping her breath and curling her toes in her slippers. It was over before she could respond, but his mouth had been hot enough to brand, turning her inside out.

He straightened and his gaze delved into hers before she could hide the yearning he had provoked. With a final caress of his thumb against her cheek, he left.

His absence always left her bereft, no matter how much she hated herself for being dependent on him, but there was more. She felt as though he'd just promised to fight for her, which was deeply heartening after she'd pretty much given up on his wanting anything to do with her.

Maybe that was wishful thinking, though.

"He reminds me of Enrique's father," Sorcha murmured after Alessandro was gone. She rocked gently. They'd both been given slings so the babies were tucked securely against them in case they nodded off in their comfortable gliding rockers.

"How so?" Octavia asked, curious how any man could be anything like Alessandro. In every way, he was a step above anyone she had ever met.

"His way of taking control. So confident and determined. You're lucky to have him here. I guess we both are," she said wryly.

"Your husband isn't here?" Octavia probed gently, wanting to know more about her new friend. Well, she hoped they were becoming friends. She had lost touch with the few women she'd known in Naples. They'd never been true friends anyway, just young women she'd gone to school with, most of them single and keen to party, hunting in packs for Mr. Right. After she married and became pregnant and moved to London, Octavia had had nothing in common with them. They'd moved on without her.

"He's in Spain," Sorcha answered, voice growing

strained. "There was an accident." She lifted a quick hand from the back of her baby's head, staying Octavia's quick gasp. "He's fine. Recovered. Mostly. But no, he isn't here."

"Because you delivered early? Is he on his way?" Octavia asked, instinctively trying to comfort.

Sorcha's mouth pulled down at the corners and her gaze skimmed the nursery. Only one nurse remained and she was on the telephone.

"We're not married. Not together," Sorcha admitted, offering a brave, but flat smile. It fell away very quickly, as though she was having second thoughts about confessing that she was single. As though it was a crime to be ashamed of.

"I'm sorry," Octavia said thinly, worried she'd overstepped. "But you won't leave here without my phone number," she added on impulse. "You and I are in this together."

"Seems so, doesn't it?" Sorcha said with a flash of her pretty smile. "Mum always tells me there's a silver lining to any of life's setbacks. I'll be going home to stay with her in Ireland until I'm ready to go back to work, though. I won't be here to have coffee in person. We'll have to do it over the tablet."

"Oh," Octavia said, crestfallen. As much as she'd been yearning to go back to Naples all these months, now that she'd seen Alessandro again, she wasn't sure. He might be taking her side right now, but where had he been all these months?

Funny how she'd thought marriage would offer her a chance at a real family, but she felt more alone than ever, despite having a child with him.

"A friend over the tablet would be better than none at all," Octavia assured her.

* * *

Alessandro was used to results. If they weren't provided promptly, he got them himself, which was what he was doing right now.

He stationed one of his bodyguards at the nursery door and the other accompanied him and the administrator through the green corridors to meet the hospital's head of security, Gareth Underwood. Underwood was burly with a fringe of closely cropped hair that left the top of his head bald. He wore wire-rim glasses and a shirt in the particular shade of beige that marked a man as uniformly practical. An access card was clipped to his chest pocket and a radio hung off his hip.

He cocked his head as he shook Alessandro's hand. "Mrs. Ferrante's husband," he repeated. "You're aware that your cousin identified himself as her husband last night?"

That news was not as surprising as it should be and more than a little irritating. After several escapades in their teens, including one that had even left him making explanations to the law, Alessandro had given Primo strict instructions never to take his identity for any reason. Today, however, he wound up making excuses.

"An effort to ensure her safety, I'm sure. Without going into detail, we've had some security concerns at home in Italy." The possibility had been dancing in Alessandro's subconscious that this baby switch could be an open attack from the faceless threat he'd been trying to identify for months. He refused to man panic stations until he had all the facts, though. For now, "Octavia was supposed to deliver at a private clinic where her security was already arranged. Primo was only looking out for her, I'm sure."

"And she didn't go to the private clinic because...?" Gareth prompted.

"The ambulance failed to arrive and her labor progressed very quickly." That still infuriated him, but he kept a firm cap on himself. "They had to bring her here."

"I looked into that." The administrator held up his cell phone. "Dispatch confirms no other ambulance was called to that address, just the one that brought her here. She made that call herself."

"Obviously dispatch didn't log Primo's request," Alessandro stated tightly, deeply disturbed that his wife had suffered needlessly. "I'll follow up with them. None of us would be here if the ambulance had come when ordered and taken her to the correct hospital."

"Sir?" A wiry technician invited them into a control room. It was small and hot, as these types of stations usually were, and a tight fit for all of them. They were quickly shown an image of Primo trying to accompany Octavia's stretcher into a locked-down area. The nurse shook her head, pointed at her cap and scrubs, then indicated something down the hall.

"She's telling him to wait in the lounge," the administrator provided.

Seconds later, the staff was clearly under pressure, moving quickly as the emergency deliveries were stacked up. People came and went through electronically controlled doors, leaving the doors hovering open again and again. Primo took advantage and stepped into the restricted area directly outside the theaters.

Everyone looked to Alessandro.

He shrugged jerkily, wanting to explain his cousin's trespass as concern for Octavia, but finding himself holding his tongue and watching, waiting to see what Primo did next.

The technician flicked screens and a moment later they could see the interior of the restricted area. An administration desk was set up with a computer and printer. The surgeon walked out of one theater, peeling scrubs as she went. She threw them into a bin and quickly began to wash her hands. There was no sound, but the way she pointed toward the door with her elbow suggested she was ordering Primo to leave, but she was being urged into the other theater and hurried to put on fresh scrubs and comply.

When a nurse came bustling from the first theater, she halted with surprise, but Primo pointed to the room labeled Theater Two. Whatever he said seemed to alleviate the nurse's concern. She was in a hurry. She grabbed a tiny striped cap from a cupboard, then quickly began preparing two trays with papers and pens and…

"Name tags?" Alessandro guessed as he saw a printed strip go onto each tray.

"With the mother's name and the bar code that matches her file," the administrator clarified. "They print them ahead when they can and add the time of birth in the theater."

Another nurse came out of Theater Two. She examined both trays, drew one closer to herself, then was pulled into a hunt for something with the other nurse.

That was when Primo glanced at the closed-circuit camera eye, shifted his back to block the line of sight to the trays and made a furtive movement.

"Stop it right there," Underwood ordered.

Alessandro was aware that they were all looking at him, but he couldn't take his eyes off the frozen image. He shook his head, unwilling to believe what they were suspecting. What *he* suspected.

"He wouldn't," he told them, but doubt had arrived as irrevocably as the stork.

Knowledge, really. Cold recognition that all the small steps he'd taken to keep the Ferrante family cohesive and successful had snapped at its weakest link: his determination to believe in his cousin's unwavering loyalty.

The tape was restarted and each nurse briskly took her tray into the separate theaters.

"You said it was procedure to check them against the mother's in the delivery room," Alessandro recalled, trying to remain rational while adrenaline ballooned in his system, pressing him to go on the attack.

The hospital administrator flattened his lips into a grim line. "Normally, I'd guarantee it would be read aloud and checked by two nurses, but there was a lot of pressure on the staff last night. Those are the sorts of conditions when corners are cut and oversights happen."

"He couldn't have known they'd both be boys, though," Underwood said. "If one had been born a girl…"

"He knew Octavia was having a boy," Alessandro said tightly. Deep in his subconscious, Primo's assurance that he would look after Octavia while she was in London took on a malevolent undertone. Alessandro had spent a lifetime trying to be understanding, elevating Primo to the highest position beneath him as recompense for not holding this one, but Primo's consistent acts of competition now rose with snaking heads of acrimony and envy and treachery.

"The Kelly baby was already born. The first nurse took out a cap for him," he heard the administrator say through the pounding in his ears.

The truth was pummeling like stones against Alessandro's chest and shoulders and between his eyes. Primo had betrayed him.

While deep down, a part of him wondered if Primo's treachery was justified. The guilt of causing his own father's death had never left Alessandro. He'd always taken Primo's challenges as his due. His punishment. He believed he should be constantly tested to prove his worth.

He had tried to make up for the terrible actions that had cost his father's life, though. The patriarch would still have been running things if not for Sandro's burst of temper. As reparation, he always set the family's needs above his own. He would lay down his life for the Ferrantes.

To be attacked so gravely from within, through his wife and child, was a greater penalty than he was willing to pay, however.

"I'd like to talk to your cousin," Underwood said.

In a deadly tone, Alessandro said, "So would I."

CHAPTER FOUR

ALESSANDRO CAME BACK wearing a look she'd never seen, as if he was a warrior cast in bronze. On the surface he seemed remote, but he radiated such danger Octavia closed her arms protectively around their baby.

"Did you learn anything?" she asked, already over-wrought, but needing to know. The sense of threat he projected tightened her throat, as if her body knew on a visceral level that he was in a lethal mood and she should be very still and quiet and not risk drawing his notice.

But he knew exactly where she was. His gaze caught at hers and drilled. The banked ember of fury in his eyes pushed her back in her chair.

It's not my fault, she wanted to cry.

"They're still questioning everyone." His voice was both devoid of inflection, yet terrifyingly harsh. "I'll be leaving with the administrator to see Primo."

Good luck, Octavia almost said, but she always kept her opinions about Primo to herself. Even if he'd seen something, he would only speak up if he saw a benefit to his own situation. More likely he'd somehow turn this into her causing trouble for nothing. Fear of what he might say layered atop her exhaustion and despair, crinkling her brow and making her bite her lips.

"What are you thinking?" Alessandro demanded.

She started at the caustic edge on his tone. Since when did he notice she had any thoughts at all?

"Nothing." She had to work to meet his eyes, disturbed to see he was watching her so closely. She didn't want him seeing her animosity toward his cousin, though. She knew how close he and Primo were and didn't want to create even more of an obstacle in their marriage.

Not that she lived with Alessandro. She lived with his mother and, quite ironically, thought Ysabelle was rather nice, despite all her gushing displays and disregard of propriety. Octavia wished the woman spent more time at her home in London, rather than hunting husbands on the Côte d'Azur.

So much left unspoken. It was disheartening if she thought about it, and made the future seem very bleak.

"Try to relax," Alessandro said gruffly. "You're safe here." His hard voice and flat mouth belied what he was saying. "The hospital is bringing in extra security for the entire floor. So am I. Each baby will have a guard of his own until this is sorted out and so will you and Sorcha."

Sorcha looked up at her name and Octavia wondered whether Enrique's father was capable of this kind of dispassionate lockdown of lives. Did he also bury frightening news in the guise of comfort? Octavia was introspective, not stupid.

"You think this was deliberate." Her limbs drained of feeling and her heart slowed to clumsy, disjointed bumps. *"Who—?"*

She looked to Sorcha, thoughts flying to who could possibly want to attack such a nice woman in such a subversive, evil way?

But the grim way Alessandro kept his gaze on her and Lorenzo told Octavia that Sorcha wasn't the target. *She* was. They were.

All the air in her lungs dried up, leaving her sipping for oxygen.

"We have your blood types," the administrator said, glancing up from a clipboard as he addressed both mothers. "I'd like to give you the results, even though they're not conclusive."

Not conclusive? Octavia instinctively cradled Lorenzo closer. The babies now wore additional tags reading Baby One and Baby Two, but this was her son.

"Ironically," the administrator said, "we should have labeled the boys A and B, since that is the blood type they've come back with." He smiled faintly.

"I'm a B. That was confirmed, *si*?" Alessandro said swiftly. His hawk-like gaze swooped onto Lorenzo with an avid light, making Octavia wonder if he'd been holding back attaching to his child until he knew irrefutably that this boy was his.

An electric jolt went through her as she sensed him reaching out in a preternatural claim in that moment. Recognizing. Accepting. It was bittersweet because it came on the heels of something dark and nefarious that he wasn't sharing with her. If only she knew him well enough to see beneath that granite-like mask he wore.

"You are a B, Mr. Ferrante. And your wife is an A," the administrator said, gaze on the form. "Ms. Kelly is an O and the baby she holds is A. At the moment, none of you can be ruled out as a parent for either of these infants. If Mr. Montero comes up as an A, however, we can rule out his fathering this baby." He nodded at Lorenzo.

"Did you call him?" Octavia swung her attention to Sorcha, even though she hadn't seen her new friend use a phone. But she was ready to beg. In some ways it didn't matter to Octavia who had caused this misery or why, they both just needed their beliefs confirmed so they could move on with mothering in peace.

"We've been in touch with Mr. Montero," the administrator said smoothly. "He was heading straight to the clinic and his results should be with us shortly."

"Wait. What? You called *Cesar*?" Sorcha screeched.

The results came from Spain while Alessandro was still out. What the mothers had known instinctively, science had proven. The babies would be kept in the hospital until the DNA tests confirmed it, but everyone accepted that Lorenzo was hers and Enrique belonged to Sorcha.

Both she and Sorcha slumped in relief and Octavia finally returned to her room—where a bouquet the size of Sicily had been delivered with a card that read, "I'll be with you as soon as I can, A."

And yet he was still with Primo.

That bitter reality kept her awake despite her exhaustion. *We have a baby*, she mentally shouted. *Don't you care?* She had texted the blood test results, had seen the notification that her message had been read, but all she heard back was radio silence.

She might as well be Sorcha, raising her baby alone.

The thought sliced a kind of agony through her, but she couldn't keep doing this, either: waiting for Prince Sandro to arrive on his steed to make her feel worthy.

What she needed was to work on her self-esteem. It had never been particularly strong. Her childhood had been one of strict rules and sighs of tested tolerance, impelling her to press herself hard into the mold her parents wanted just to earn a shred of approval.

She might have kicked up at boarding school, but that had been as much about trying to fit in as proving to her parents she wasn't under their thumb. By nature she was the bookish sort, so hanging with the party crowd, pretending she was into boys and fashion and drinking hadn't felt right in the first place, but she'd loved the sense of freedom and independence in making risky decisions: sneaking out of her room at night, voicing strong opinions without caring what anyone thought of them.

Then someone had slipped her something and she would have been one more assault statistic, no doubt, if the party she was at hadn't been discovered by the faculty as she was passing out. Having her stomach pumped and being suspended for a few weeks had almost been a relief at that point, becoming an excuse to eschew the rowdy crowd and their superficial pursuits if she wanted to return to school.

She had toed the line after that, scared of that spark of insurgence inside her, learning to get by with her own company and buckling to her father's dictates because it felt safer than trusting her wild side. Eventually she'd attached loosely to a group of girls from Naples because they had geography in common, but she didn't have a history of fancy vacations or brushes with celebrity to turn into engaging stories. She definitely didn't have shocking sexual exploits to share.

The identity of her husband had been the first thing to cause ripples of reaction—mostly admiration—among her shallow social pool. To this day, Octavia didn't understand why Alessandro had chosen her. She was supposed to have married Primo.

She thought back to that gala when she'd met the two men, searching for clues to what he'd seen in her when she'd been such a generic example of an heiress.

"That's the man your father invited," her mother had said, pointing out Primo. "The one he thinks might accept you. He would love a connection like the Ferrante family."

"The one on the right?" Octavia had asked, intimidated

and alarmed as she glanced toward the two men, both thirtyish. Primo's boyish good looks hadn't even registered beside the compelling Alessandro's carved features and arrogant sweep of his stern gaze around the room.

"The left," her mother had said. "The taller one is his cousin, the head of the family. He controls Ferrante Imprese Internazionali. He doesn't look very approving, does he? I wonder if that's why he's here, to decide if we measure up."

He didn't look approving at all, Octavia had silently agreed, intimidated by his air of censure. She told herself she was relieved her father wasn't aiming so high as to think Alessandro Ferrante would be interested. The second-in-command, Primo, would be enough of a coup. He looked arrogant in a different way. Smug almost.

"Make a good impression," her mother had ordered.

Blowing out a surreptitious breath, Octavia had tried to imagine how one made a positive impression on a potential husband. It was the first time she was being forced to try, but she'd said she would marry the man they chose, so try she would.

Her father had introduced her to the men a few minutes later. Primo had looked her up and down like a buyer at an auction considering a broodmare. Alessandro waited for her gaze to come up to his and locked the contact into something unbreakable.

His air of dissatisfaction was stronger up close. The way he dourly took in every detail from her upswept hair, to the shade of her lipstick, to the scoop of her neckline across her breasts, suggested he was searching for flaws.

Her insides quivered under his inspection while she found herself holding her breath, waiting for his verdict.

"We should dance," Primo had said in a hard voice, his words coming from off to the right. His hand had come out in her periphery, but she'd been unable to drag her gaze from the frosted moss of Alessandro's irises.

Something flashed in Alessandro's eyes as she turned her body to follow Primo without turning her head, only releasing her from her enthrallment when he broke their stare to ask her father something.

She had no recollection of what she and Primo had talked about while they danced, but she could remember every word and intonation of her conversation with Alessandro a little later, when he'd found her on the terrace off the hotel ballroom.

She'd excused herself to the powder room then slipped out there to escape disturbing thoughts of maybe *not* going through with an arranged marriage. It was cold feet, she told herself. The reality of what she had agreed to was hitting her with the meeting of a potential husband, but that didn't mean all the reasons she'd accepted as good ones suddenly became bad, she tried telling herself.

She shivered. It was cool. No one else was out here, but it was pretty. The boat lights were streaked like finger paint on the rippling water of the Golfo di Napoli and she was always most comfortable with her own company.

Yet oddly not annoyed when Alessandro intruded.

He brought her champagne, asking, "How long have you known Primo?"

She shivered again, this time less from the chilly air, and more from a preternatural wariness of such a dynamic man. They touched glass rims and murmured, *"Salud."*

"I just met him tonight," she replied.

He paused on the way to taking his first sip, gaze still locked to hers. "Talking to your father, it sounds like they've had several meetings already." Grimness edged his tone.

She choked a little as the bubbles went the wrong way

and burned her throat. It wasn't that she was surprised. Not really. Her father had made it clear all her life that he expected her to marry the man he chose for her, but she would have thought she would be consulted earlier in the process.

"You didn't know that," he guessed.

"No," she murmured. But since one of her father's other expectations was that she not question his decisions, she kept her reaction to that one disturbed response.

She had felt Alessandro's gaze on her profile and her heart had pounded as though she'd run up a thousand flights of stairs. This was just a test, she'd told herself. He was a rich and powerful man heading a very rich and powerful family. He wanted to know if she—if her family—was worthy of joining his. She needed to be her most pleasant and conciliatory, reassure him that she'd make a fine wife for his cousin, but her throat could barely work to swallow, let alone make conversation.

"You're willing to go through with an arranged marriage?" he asked. "You wouldn't prefer a love match?"

Did he think she was gold digging?

"An arranged marriage makes sense to me," she said, reminding herself as she spoke, even though her voice wasn't quite steady. Until tonight, she hadn't met a man who attracted her enough to consider the alternative.

Not that she would really consider a love match. She didn't think of herself as the sort men fell for. She'd also been raised under the attitude that her uterus was the center of her worth, and only then if it delivered a healthy heir who could grow up to take possession of her father's fortune. She didn't *believe* that, but given her mother's struggle to produce her, Octavia couldn't help feel a duty to make her sacrifice worthwhile. She had agreed to follow through with her parents' plans and hopefully, finally, earn their appreciation.

"Most women I know want to marry a man who is well positioned, but they try to find them in bars and at parties. Men at parties want to hook up, not settle down." Octavia had watched hearts get tossed to and fro as her female acquaintances tried to make these potential mates fall in love and propose. It hadn't seemed worth the heartache when all she really wanted was children. "There's a disconnect."

She glanced at him, thinking she sounded as if she was showing off, using fancy words. It disconcerted her to see she had his full attention.

"I want to have a family so why shouldn't I let my parents find a good prospect to father my children? One who could provide well for them?" she finished in a mumble into her glass.

"You've given this a lot of thought," he said.

She hadn't wanted to do anything to jeopardize the negotiation, but she'd taken offense, challenging tartly, "It's my future. Why wouldn't I?"

"I'm not criticizing. Believe me, I'm impressed. I'd prefer an arranged marriage myself."

Her heart had skipped under what sounded like a compliment. She searched his expression in the silvery moonlight, catching an impression of computation, as if he was realigning certain facts and developing a fresh strategy.

"Do you intend to run your father's portfolio after you marry? Is that why you're letting him choose your husband?"

As if her father would allow that! Mario had grudgingly yielded to her desire to finish school, disparaging her study of psychology and sociology, then had confined her work in his office to redecorating his lobby where he had consistently pulled rank on final decisions. She'd thought about striking out, taking a job elsewhere, but despite a dozen find-your-career quizzes she'd never identified anything that had sparked her enthusiasm enough to defy her father over it.

"My father has traditional views on a woman's place," she said dispassionately.

"Which doesn't answer my question."

"I thought I did," she'd said truthfully. "Your own family's fortune is managed by men, isn't it?"

"Not entirely. I have three female cousins who head different departments. My sister runs an architecture firm I co-own with her and her husband, and my middle sister has a string of boutiques that I underwrote quite confidently. They're all very successful, so I'm well aware that women make perfectly capable executives."

His lack of sexism was refreshing, but if his remarks were meant to encourage her, they had had the opposite effect, making her think she wasn't trying hard enough to reach her potential.

"If your cousin needed me to take on some of the management, of course I would be willing to learn," she had assured him with manufactured confidence. "At least until children come along." Octavia's mother had been there, but she hadn't *been there*. Octavia would do both. "But I'm sure my father will remain active in the role for a long time, so…"

She trailed off, heart snagged by a new look of intention in his gaze.

"What?" she prompted.

"I've had an idea." A faint smile drifted across his lips—lips that were a sensual contrast against the rest of his starkly hewed features. His cheeks were hollow, his chin strong, his expression vaguely dismissive of what she'd just said. Reaching out, he'd stolen her champagne and set both glasses on the narrow rail. "Let's dance, Octavia."

He'd taken hold of her hand and tugged her back into the ballroom, his calm surety causing a wild chaos inside her. To this day, she could feel the way his hands had burned her through her gown, already taking on the possessive quality she had grown to revel in.

Across the room, where her parents stood with Primo, her mother was waiting to catch her eye to signal that Octavia should rejoin them.

"I think they want to talk to us," she said.

Alessandro had continued dancing, saying almost casually, "What if my cousin was not your potential husband, Octavia? What if I was? Would you still rather be a full-time wife devoted to running our home life, which I'd prefer, I must admit, or would I have a part-time business partner whom I would sleep with, which I would settle for?"

"Are you serious?" She'd misstepped, forcing him to catch her close to keep her upright. The press of his body had flushed hers with sexual awareness—something that had never happened to her before. The heated glow had risen up and radiated outward from her center like an aura, sensitizing her skin, warming her cheeks, encasing her in a blush of excitement.

Something happened to him in the same instant. He flashed a look of reassessment at her, brows crashing together as though he'd been taken completely by surprise. For a moment, his hands tightened on her and a muscle ticked in his cheek. A question hung in the balance, but she didn't know what that question was.

Only that his mouth tightened with resolve as he made up his mind.

"Wh-why would you want to marry me?" she asked.

"As I said, I'd prefer a practical arrangement myself. I'll need an heir and your father's assets are a good mix for ours. Did you respond like this when you danced with Primo?" His thumb had traced a circle against her rib cage, the caress tiny and mind-blowing at the same time as he kept her pinned to his front.

"What? No!" Heat like she'd never known had flamed upward, burning her throat and stinging her cheeks. It was both embarrassment that they were talking so bluntly and reaction, pure animal attraction.

For the first time, she saw he was capable of humor as he flashed a grin of amused satisfaction.

"Good," he said with a heavy-lidded look that put a funny knot in her belly. "And I'm glad you respond to me. It will make the making of those babies you want more fun for both of us."

Lying in her hospital bed, Octavia threw her arm over her eyes, flooded with the same painful excitement and callow embarrassment now as had overwhelmed her then. What had he ever seen in her but naivety and willingness to be bedded?

As they'd resumed the dance, he'd kept his jaw angled proudly to look across the bobbing heads around them toward his cousin, asking almost casually, "Well?"

All she'd been able to think was that this wasn't the man her father had chosen. She shouldn't refuse Primo, but what if she landed a better catch? Such a lofty aspiration, she thought now with bitterness, but at the time she'd experienced a funny rush of excitement. It wasn't rebellion if it was *improvement*.

Was he really asking her to marry him?

In case she was misinterpreting things, she merely answered the question he'd asked first. "I would prefer to focus on building a good home life after I marry."

The aspiration was stark and fervent, actually. She'd had the same banked ache all her life. She wanted a place in the world that was *hers*. A place where she was welcomed and loved. Surely if she was a better mother than her own, her children would love her? *That* was her real dream. To be loved.

"I'll speak to your father and begin working out the details." His voice provoked the most delicious bubble of tension in her.

But she'd been surprised enough to halt again. Her skirt had swayed around both their legs. "Are you serious? We've only just met."

"You've only just met Primo. But you've chosen me."

She swallowed. Had she? When? This was starting to feel too fast. Impulsive.

"What…? What about him?" she asked.

Something fierce flashed in his expression, but he'd suppressed it before she fully caught what it could have been. "I'll handle my cousin."

He'd returned her to her parents, saying to Primo, "We need to talk."

Primo had given her another hard study, as if he was trying to find what he'd missed, then set his jaw and left with Alessandro.

"You ruined it," her father had growled in accusation.

"You were on the balcony with his cousin?" her mother scolded. "He was asking for you."

"Nothing happened," Octavia protested, but a lot had. "I mean, not like anything *wrong*." She had been quivering in a kind of shock. "We just talked and… I think he's going to offer for me. Alessandro, I mean." It sounded outlandish even to her, now that he was gone.

Her father had given her a grim look. "You misunderstood," he insisted. What could Alessandro possibly want with her, his disdainful sneer had asked?

What *did* Alessandro want from her? Compliance? A son? Would he be happy now? Approve?

In every way, Alessandro was so much more than she was. She'd realized it that night on the terrace and it had only become more apparent as time wore on. He had more education and street smarts, pulled all the strings, had the power and the influence and confidence in his own prowess whether it was in negotiating the marriage contract or teaching his wife the ways of their marital bed.

All she'd had was youthful, twenty-two-year-old looks that were passably pretty because she'd made a concerted study of how to highlight her assets and downplay her flaws. She prided herself on things like duty and loyalty because they were the only things her parents had ever valued and she'd overshot independence, skinning her knees hard enough to scare her back into her mother's lap.

She had been a complete doormat.

It had to stop.

Alessandro had been exhausted when the interrogation was finished, but he was drawn to the hospital rather than bed, still poised to fight—because his cousin had attacked him in a very selective, devious way. Gone were the pesky one-upmanship salvos. This had very nearly succeeded in causing unimaginable damage.

It had nearly cost Octavia's and Lorenzo's lives.

A storm of retaliation was gathered in his chest, threatening to burst the civilized armor he had welded around himself with careful precision after his immature, hair-trigger temper had snuffed out his father's life in the time it took to blow. Since then, he had learned to contain the wild force inside him so, even though he wanted to do violence to Primo, he ruthlessly disciplined himself to seek reprisal through legal channels. He would pursue every avenue of justice open to him and he would lose nothing in this undeclared war Primo had subversively raged against him.

Walking away unscathed would be his ultimate revenge.

He checked on Lorenzo, having already learned from Octavia that her instinct had been right. This was their son. Alessandro could barely take in the magnitude of how easily he could have missed knowing his own flesh and blood.

Those thoughts fed his rage so he pushed them aside, going to Octavia's room where he was relieved to find her asleep. He wasn't ready to talk about all that had transpired today.

Part of him was tempted to crawl into the bed alongside her, which he put down to his naturally possessive nature. Having a woman in his bed was something he'd always enjoyed for the obvious reason, but his need to hold her was a more primal compulsion. Protective, certainly, but an assertion of his right, too. Octavia was his and, despite Primo's plotting, would remain so.

Her recent surgery gave him the strength to show some decency, though. She needed her rest and he wanted her to have it.

Somehow he had disturbed her, however, because he'd barely dozed off when she awoke, pulling away from his light fingers against the pulse in her wrist, giving him an inscrutable look he could barely read in the filtered city light that slid past the vertical blinds.

"I didn't mean to wake you," he said, hearing the rasp of fatigue in his voice.

"What time is it? I should check on Lorenzo, see if he's hungry." She tried to push herself to sit.

"I was just in there." He leaned forward to touch her shoulder, feeling her stiffen under the weight of his fingertips. It wasn't the first time she'd reacted with something like rejection, which disturbed him. "He was sleeping," he said, pretending he hadn't noticed, offering a reassuring caress that she retreated from by dropping onto her back. "The nurse said she'd come for you when he wakes."

"Oh." She licked her lips. Her mouth looked shiny and pouty. Very delectable. He'd kissed her earlier, but it hadn't been the right moment for the kind of reunion he craved. Right now wasn't any better. His sharpest male instincts were activated, desperate not only to go on the attack in his role as protector, but wanting a private expression between them that affirmed his role as the chosen one to kiss and touch and cover her. He wanted the physical claiming that reinforced their bond.

Not possible, obviously. Not in her condition. He hoped that was the only reason she was tensing under his touch.

"How are you feeling?" he asked, genuinely wanting to know, but his voice thickened involuntarily as frustration bled back into him. Primo had risked her life and Lorenzo's by failing to call the ambulance. How had he thought to get away with that along with the rest? He couldn't think of any of it without nearly losing what temper he'd managed to keep.

"I'm fine," she murmured, shifting to draw the light blanket over her arms and shoulders, all the way up to her chin.

A lie, of course. She couldn't possibly be fine. He wondered why she wasn't being honest with him. The estrangement he'd been sensing took on new dimensions as he grasped how much power Primo had had, moving into Alessandro's mother's mansion under a guise of waiting out renovations. It had seemed insignificant when Primo had asked Alessandro's mother four months ago if he could prevail on her. Sandro hadn't seen any harm in it so he hadn't interfered, but now…

Now he saw it as the seemingly innocuous chess move it had been.

"You're not fine, Octavia. We've both had a number of shocks and there's more. Primo switched the babies' name tags."

Primo. Perhaps she'd guessed it subconsciously, but hadn't wanted to face it because it was too cruel a thing for one person to do to another, especially to an innocent like Sorcha and a pair of newborn babies.

"I didn't realize he hated me that much," she said.

"It wasn't you he hated," Alessandro said, rising abruptly, shrugging within the collared shirt he'd changed into. He still hadn't shaved, though. He turned to pace across the end of her bed, then stood at the window, angled to see out the slats of the blinds.

The disillusionment he projected affected her, making her heart pang even though she didn't want to be softhearted Octavia anymore, the one who thought she could keep herself safe and ease tension between her parents by doing as she was told.

"Who then? You?" she croaked. "I'm the one who chose you over him. He never forgave me for it." Why were there always such harsh consequences when she asserted herself?

Alessandro swung around. "He said that?"

She debated a moment. The cousins had always been so close it had been yet one more wall that had kept her from trespassing anywhere near Alessandro's deeper self. He wouldn't want to hear anything against his precious Primo.

"Not in so many words, but it was obvious. He thought it was my fault he was stuck in London and said he should have told my father where to go when he first approached him about joining the family fortunes. It was clear he was angry and I gave up trying to make amends. But I didn't realize he was capable of something this awful."

"I needed him here in London. I planned that before we even met. I didn't think he could do something like this, either," Alessandro bit out, giving his face a tired rub. "But he was directing his anger with me onto you. He's always been jealous. Ever since my father died and my grandfather and uncle turned their attention to grooming me to run things. He felt passed over."

She knew the basics of their family history, that Alessandro had been twelve when he lost his father. His grandfather, Ermanno, had already been semiretired. Alessandro's mother and her children had moved into the *castello* with Ermanno so he could mentor Alessandro himself. Alessandro's uncle Giacomo, Primo's father, had taken over the day-to-day running of things until Alessandro was old enough to do it himself.

"Primo's father was in charge for a decade, about as long as my own father was. He's always believed he has as much right to take over as I do. We fought about it more than once in our teens. Quite honestly, if my grandfather had seen Primo as the better leader, he would have named him the successor, but Primo was always driven by passion and not in the right way. I thought we had put it to rest when I gave him this position in London. He had the freedom to grow the branch under his own terms. I believed his loyalty was unshakeable."

The disillusioned note in his voice almost made her sympathize, but she resented his blind belief at the same time.

"That's why *I* trusted him," she said. His misjudgment had shaken her belief in him and thus her belief in herself. She'd never had much faith in her parents beyond the expectation that they would keep her fed and physically safe, but Alessandro had seemed to offer more than that. Then he had delivered…this.

She never should have counted on him. But she had.

"*Did* you trust him? Because you told the paramedics you didn't want him near you or the baby," he said pointedly.

"It seemed paranoid when I said it." She was reluctant even now to admit how much a victim she'd come to feel around Primo. He'd been downright sinister catching her in those first contractions and saying with such concern, "*Go lie down. I'll call the hospital.*" Who imagined anyone would lie about something like that? It was only as things had progressed, as fear for her life and her baby's had gripped her, that she'd started to suspect he was deliberately delaying things.

"What could he possibly have thought to gain by doing something like this?" The magnitude of the crime kept striking like aftershocks from a quake.

"It wasn't something he planned," he said with grim cast to his hard features. "The opportunity presented and he acted. He admitted that much. A paternity question down the road would have caused us a great deal of suffering and could have opened doors to his own heir taking control over my false one. That's as far as he got with thinking it through."

"*Mio Dio,*" she breathed, sliding her arm up over her eyes, hiding from the thought of Alessandro questioning her faithfulness a year from now, when they might have discovered the baby wasn't his.

Suddenly Alessandro's voice was right beside her. "He was behind some death threats I received earlier this year."

"What?" she gasped, dropping her arm.

"I didn't tell you because you were already anxious about the pregnancy. I wanted you near the specialists here in London anyway, but it seemed safer for you to be out of Naples. That's why I haven't brought you home, even to visit." His jaw looked carved from marble.

"All this because he's *jealous*? No, he was punishing me," she said with an appalled crack in her voice.

"He wasn't happy about our marriage, that's true. Had he married you and been given control of your father's fortune, he would have been in a better position to challenge me over controlling the family company. When I married you, I became untouchable. There really was no other way for him to bring me down except to attack my personal life."

"That's sick," she said, recoiling. "Did you know that? That his reasons for talking with my father were more about making a strategic move against you than wanting a wife?"

A very brief pause, then, "I was aware there could be certain challenges if he bettered his position," he said carefully. Too carefully.

"You married me to prevent him from gaining an advantage," she breathed. She hadn't thought she could be any more shocked, but she was. All those tiny details she'd recalled from that first evening took on new meaning. His initial air of disapproval— "You were planning to stop it, one way or another." His question about whether she wanted a love match… "You wanted to talk me out of it, but you proposed instead. It was a calculated move to keep him in his place."

"It was a precaution," he said. "I wanted to marry eventually, and you and I were well suited."

"No, we weren't! Not if this was the real reason you proposed!"

"Don't get upset—"

"I *am* upset!" she said in such a burst, her stomach hurt.

"Octavia, calm down." He sounded so patronizing she wanted to smack him. "Today was very stressful and you've just had surgery. Let it all sink in and tomorrow you'll have a clearer view."

"He tried to take our *baby* because you took the wife he wanted," she stressed. "Why aren't *you* upset?"

"I am." The words snapped like a flag in a stiff breeze, but he didn't look or sound upset. But then, this was a man who had approached marriage so cold-bloodedly, she couldn't even let herself think of it yet. "But you don't have to worry about him ever again. The police have taken him for further questioning. The hospital is pressing charges for interfering with the baby tags and I will make a formal complaint when we get back to Naples for the death threats. He will be too tied up in legal proceedings to bother us and certainly won't have a place in our lives or any sort of position in the corporation. We'll put all of this behind us very quickly."

She stared at him, stupefied at how easily he thought this could be shaken off like dirt from a rug. It was something her parents would have done. *The puppy was a nuisance, Octavia. Those old books were in the way. That friend of yours needn't visit again once school finishes.*

You're just a marble I won from my cousin, Octavia.

Discussion over. Move on.

She wanted to curl up into a ball and cry, but she had a son to think of. Failing to fight for a better situation had nearly cost her the chance to raise him herself. She couldn't afford to be acquiescent. Not anymore.

"I'm not going back to Naples with you," she said firmly.

CHAPTER FIVE

"But that's where our son will be. Surely you'd prefer to be with him?"

He shouldn't have said it. He'd been down to his last vibrating nerve, already feeling so guilty his self-respect had been consigned to the London sewer. Her refusal to come home with him had snapped his leash. He'd seen himself losing what Primo had tried to cost him and he'd reacted with the sort of ruthless aggression he'd been suppressing all day.

He would *not* let his cousin win.

Octavia had stared at him in stunned, hurt silence, her face the furthest thing from the amenable expression he was used to seeing there. Beneath her crushed anguish, her eyes had blazed with singular fury. Raw emotion that had sparked off his own.

For a moment he'd scented the fight he was itching for.

Then a cool contempt had flickered in her face before she'd rolled onto her side and closed her eyes.

It had taken everything in him not to wrench the rail from her bed and drag her around to continue hashing things out, but the nurse had come in. Lorenzo was hungry.

Octavia left without a backward glance and didn't return.

Why the hell had he allowed himself to lash out like that?

He'd managed to hold his temper for hours in his

mother's sitting room, as the police had pulled one vile act of insurgence after another from Primo. His cousin's resentment had festered here in London, to the point where he'd taken pleasure in torturing Alessandro by recounting the way Octavia had begged for her husband while she writhed in labor, sweating and scared.

"Does that bother you, Sandro? I'm surprised. You only married her to stop me from doing it."

Not entirely true. He had had a clear view of the board when a chance remark from their accounting VP had tipped Alessandro off to Primo's contemplation of marriage. Alessandro *had* gone to that charity gala in search of ammunition to protest the union and circumvent any power plays Primo might have made.

Perhaps he should have acknowledged the seeds of his own mistrust then, but he hadn't seen Primo's actions as overtly aggressive, merely that if his cousin married well there was *potential* for trouble. It was Alessandro's habit to look for such signs and nip them in the bud. In all sides of his life, he forestalled the potential for damage wherever he could.

The idea of proposing to Octavia hadn't struck him until he'd talked with her on the terrace. He had gone out there to discover how determined she was to marry Primo, but marriage hadn't been on his mind. He'd always had a distant awareness that he had a duty to produce an heir at some point, but that was a future thing that he would get to when he was ready. And it wasn't as if he was waiting for a woman to steal his heart. Quite the contrary. He'd already decided to arrange a marriage when the time came.

So he hadn't felt quite ready to settle down that night. Primo had essentially forced the issue, but as it had turned out, once the idea of taking Octavia for himself had struck, it had stuck.

She had been pretty in an understated way with potential for genuine beauty. She'd also been collected and traditional and more than willing to accept the simple attachment of an arranged marriage over the more volatile love match his parents had had. She wanted children and wanted to devote herself to them. Given the demands of his work, he saw that as yet another way they were an immediate fit.

Best of all, the family wouldn't lose a lucrative partner and he had the perfect excuse for Primo. Lady's choice. He couldn't help that Octavia had fallen for him. Women did. If he was taking advantage of her inexperience and surface infatuation, well, it was for the greater good.

His only moment of doubt had come when he'd taken her to the dance floor. He'd wanted to lend an air of romance to his proposal, but also foreshadow his move to his cousin. As he had pulled Octavia into his front, however, and smelled the sweet, nutmeg scent of her hair, desire had rung through him with unexpected force.

She had reacted, too. The sparkle of her attraction toward him had been beautiful. Incendiary. Fuel to his fire and bordering on dangerous. He hadn't experienced such a rush of unbridled hunger in his life.

Given that he never allowed feelings to rule him, he'd thought for one brief moment of abandoning his plan—but no. Suddenly the idea of her marrying Primo, sleeping in his cousin's bed, had been unthinkable.

He had proceeded with his proposal, convinced he could handle the attraction. He had taken Primo aside to explain that he and Octavia had a connection that had to be elevated above dispassionate business transactions. Alessandro knew for a fact that her father had asked her which man she preferred. She'd chosen Sandro and, since he was the better prospect, so had Mario.

Arranged marriages were strategic by definition, damn it. He didn't understand why she was upset to learn his reasons now.

Because it came on the heels of Primo's vindictive betrayal, he supposed. Her trust was shaken. She was looking for reassurance and not finding it in her husband. That bothered him. He prided himself on being completely reliable.

Tomorrow, he silently promised her. They would both be calmer and capable of talking rationally. She *would* come to Naples with him.

Lorenzo was over a week old when they released her. Despite cabin fever, Octavia was a little bit sorry to be discharged. The hospital had been a nice delay against worrying over how she and Alessandro would proceed. She hadn't seen him much. He'd had meetings with police and conference calls with his grandfather and appointments with executives in the various offices. He called and texted often, but his absence had left her to explain to Sorcha and her Spaniard how the mix-up had occurred.

Cesar Montero did have a similar air of dynamic power to Alessandro's. He had been quite intimidating, arriving on a high tide of energy, sweeping into the nursery with an unequivocal demand to see his son. He was perfectly polite to Octavia—barely noticed her really, which was fine by her—but the thick tension between him and Sorcha had been like a suffocating fog.

Octavia had apologized to Sorcha when they had a moment alone, saying, "I'm so sorry this awful situation happened, Sorcha. I feel terrible—"

"Oh, I don't hold you responsible!" Sorcha reassured her, but admitted on a quivering whisper, "But Cesar didn't know about Enrique. At all." The stress of dealing with his discovery was visible in her pinched nostrils and white cheeks.

Octavia didn't judge. She was far too preoccupied with her own problems and the sordid reason her husband had married her. Part of her wanted to spill it all to her new friend, but it was so personal, so lowering.

Before she left, Sorcha made a point of exchanging contact details so they could stay in touch. "I'll be going to Spain," Sorcha had said, a conflicted expression torturing her beautiful face. "I don't expect it'll be a warm welcome from his family. I'd appreciate having a friend, even if you're in London."

"I've been in London for medical care. I live in Naples," Octavia had said, not bringing up her reservations about going back there. Alessandro hadn't said another word about their plans, but she hadn't stopped thinking about how ruthless and arrogant he'd been the other night. It hurt. She felt as if she was back in her childhood, expected to do as she was told.

And why not? She virtually always had.

"I'd like a friend, too," Octavia said with a touch more vehemence than she meant to reveal. "I'm very attached to Enrique," she added, reaching out to stroke Sorcha's son's tiny closed fist. "I'll need regular updates. I'm going to miss him. He was almost mine." It was true. She felt a strange connection to the boy.

"I feel the same," Sorcha said, eyes shining with emotion. "I'll feel so cheated, not seeing Lorenzo every day."

They hugged it out and Sorcha was gone when Alessandro settled Octavia in the back of his town car. Loneliness gripped her, keeping her silent on the short drive to his mother's mansion.

"Mother is home. She's anxious for time with Lorenzo before—" He cut himself off.

Before we leave? Was that what he had almost said?

Octavia's tender stomach muscles tightened.

His mother's mansion was a few hundred years old, its facade elegant and weathered. Inside, Ysabelle had decorated with the colorful overindulgence that matched her personality and expressive Italian roots.

As they entered, she swooped on her grandson like a gull spotting a sandwich crust, silk sleeves flowing out like wings from her bright blue dress.

Praise and endearments in rapid Italian flowed over all of them along with several embraces into clouds of an ethereal perfume, warm kisses that left lipstick stains on their cheeks and pets of the hair that made Octavia couch a smile. Alessandro was not five and didn't care to be fussed over like he was.

She didn't mind the attention. Her own mother wouldn't greet her like this, drawing her into the lounge where dozens of gifts were arranged with care on every surface, all wrapped in pastel stripes and extravagant bows.

"When did this happen?" Alessandro asked, folding his arms as he took in the grand gesture with an exasperated shake of his head.

"Surprises are fine when they're nice ones," his mother assured him, patting his arm on her way by. "Your nanny helped me," she told Octavia as she directed her into the chair with the balloons tied to the armrest.

"We have a nanny?" Octavia murmured, casting a wary glance at her husband. She didn't like surprises any more than he did.

Brianna—*call me Bree*—was young and eager and melted with adoration the moment she saw Lorenzo, but Octavia was reluctant to hand over her son to a stranger when Alessandro's threats of stealing him back to Italy were still fresh in her mind.

"You're still recovering," Alessandro said. "You need the help. I'll pitch in as much as I can, but work is completely upended right now. I have a lot of demands on my time."

Octavia hadn't considered how losing Primo would affect things at the family company. Alessandro must be putting out a lot of raging fires. The Ferrante holdings were a far-reaching and very demanding enterprise.

As she took her son from his car seat and handed the baby to his grandmother, she asked, "You really fired him?" She half expected Primo was still here and couldn't shake the tension of having to face him.

Alessandro was taken aback. "I told you he was out of our lives. Did you not believe me?"

She blinked. Not really. The men had been so close.

A hint of the torment he'd revealed that first night flickered across his expression, telling her he was still coming to terms with it all. Her heart lurched at seeing him struggle. If she'd been the type who knew how to reach out, if things hadn't been so strained between them, she might have tried to comfort him.

But she didn't know how so she only said, "Thank you," because Primo's absence lifted a giant weight off her.

"I needed my fainting couch when he told me," Ysabelle said, lowering to sit on the sofa opposite, Lorenzo in her lap. "It was such a shock."

The twist of Alessandro's mouth told Octavia that Ysabelle wasn't overstating her reaction, not that she wasn't entitled to some histrionics. Octavia was still reeling.

"Are you up to this?" Alessandro asked Octavia, jerking his head at the multitude of presents. "Or would you rather rest and open these later?"

"I can do it now. This is very nice," she told her mother-in-law. "Thank you."

"I've ordered lunch. We'll fetch you when it's ready. You can go work," Ysabelle told her son with a clasp of his hand and a kiss on the back of it. "I know that's where you'd rather be," she added with a vague scold in her tone. "Since you've already heard about my count. We're in *love*," she leaned forward to confide to Octavia. "I thought I'd never make love again and now… It's like we're nineteen!"

Alessandro sucked in a long patience-seeking breath, gaze going to the ceiling. "I will work," he said flatly. "You'll tell me if you need anything," he added with a stern look at Octavia.

She nodded, disappointed that he left, even though there was still this rock of tension sitting between them. It didn't disappear when he did, either, just gave her enough breathing room to relax and chat with her mother-in-law as she began unwrapping Lorenzo's gifts.

Octavia rose from a nap before dinner, showered and fed Lorenzo, then used her new baby monitor to listen for him as she went back to the sitting room. She was folding a little vest and placing it on the pile in the bassinet when Alessandro came in.

"The nanny can clean this up, can't she?" he said.

"I asked her to leave it out so I could look at everything again." Octavia wasn't sure why she wanted to, but it made her feel good to touch all the tiny outfits. Everything was so handsome and sweet. She held up the tuxedo on its hanger, complete with ruffled shirt, cummerbund, bow tie and black socks. "Your mother said it's for your grandfather's eightieth."

The event had been planned a year ago and until a few days ago, Octavia had had every intention of attending. Now…

She frowned, amusement falling away into a kind of despair.

Alessandro came farther into the room, bypassing the sofa to turn on the fireplace. The gas gave a low hiss and the flames leaped up, brightening the room that had turned gloomy as dusk dimmed the gray light coming through the filmy curtains.

For a moment the room seemed cheery, the mood between them intimate. Alessandro stood with one hand deep in his pocket, the other braced on the edge of the mantel, head hanging as he regarded the flames.

He was so beautiful. Like a sculpture of a Roman god come to life. And he had that gorgeous way of pursing his mouth when he was thinking, exactly as he did when he was ready to kiss her.

She swallowed.

"The police have requested we stay in London until they finalize their investigation," he said. "That will likely take us to the end of the month. I'll hold video conferences with the New York and Paris offices while I'm here, and reassign all of Primo's duties. That will give Mother plenty of time with Lorenzo and still get us home in time for my grandfather's birthday." He straightened and turned, his tone brooking no argument. "I wish we could go home sooner, but at least the staff in Naples are mine. It's the office I'm least worried about right now."

Octavia looked away, tempted to let his implacable personality roll right over her. That was the crux of the problem right there. He was such a force, so smooth in his handling of everything, she had fallen in with whatever he had suggested from minute one. *Of course I'll marry you. Anything you want. Lie down on the bed? Here?*

She'd given him her virginity, not her spine, she reminded herself, and made herself stand taller.

"I really would rather keep Lorenzo here," she managed to say with calm assertion. Away from him, she could relearn how to think for herself. "As you've pointed out, you have a lot of demands on your time. You won't see much of him anyway. At least here, he'll have his grandmother every day."

Not completely true, since Ysabelle was already talking about returning to her new lover in the south of France. Octavia forced herself to meet Alessandro's daunting gaze.

"Your parents will want to meet him," he said.

She pressed her lips together. Her father hadn't responded to her email informing him of Lorenzo's safe birth, only made a deposit of a ridiculous amount into her childhood allowance account. Her mother had sent flowers with a tag that read Congratulations. In Octavia's mind, the word had come across as deeply sarcastic.

"My parents are as capable of climbing onto an airplane as your mother is," she pointed out, tone sharpening with anger that they hadn't even called.

"Don't take out your anger toward Primo on me, Octavia," Alessandro warned in a low, dangerous tone. "You're better than that."

A disbelieving laugh escaped her while an uncomfortable rush of adrenaline burned through her limbs as the moment became a confrontation. It wasn't like her to push back, but she *had* to.

"I'm not *angry* with Primo. I hate him with every cell in my body," she corrected with a tremble in her voice. "I *am* angry with you. You left me here with him."

He absorbed that with a small rock back on his heels.

"I accept that. But I can't fire my cousin for interfering with my marriage then go home without a wife. You can imagine how things look from a distance. Some are already siding with Primo." His jaw tightened. "I can't have that kind of rift, Octavia. You and I must present a united front. You need to show you're not holding a grudge against the entire family. Together, we show everyone we are prepared to resume our lives without him and everyone will fall into line."

"You want me to pretend we're happily married," she confirmed. "Despite all that's happened." She was crushing Lorenzo's soft new jacket into a ball against her diaphragm.

"I'm not trying to downplay what he's done, but we have to move past it. We can't let it impact our marriage."

A million responses tore through her mind, but the one that came out was an incredulous, *"What marriage?"*

"We're not talking about Primo, are we?" he said grimly, expression shuttering. "You think I was dishonest about my reasons for marrying you." He folded his arms. "You're turning this into something bigger than it is, *cara*. Why I married you doesn't matter. We are married and we're going to stay that way."

This was the man she'd caught glimpses of when he spoke with other powerful men, like her father. When she had stood beside him at company events and seen minions leap to do his bidding before he'd finished stating what he wanted. No one said no to him, but she had to. *Had* to.

"Of course it doesn't matter to *you*," she corrected, blinking and trying to ignore that her eyes were stinging, hoping the low light hid how wet they were growing. "Because *I* mean nothing to you. I realize that now, thank you, although I admit it was a bit of a shock. I mean, I knew my father didn't care which Ferrante took me so long as one of you did—he's never had my best interests at heart—but I thought *you*, at least, had been more discerning. I thought you decided that night that you *liked* me, but no." It hurt so much to face that. Her voice scraped all the way up her breastbone, abrading her throat. "I didn't go into our marriage expecting love, Alessandro."

She had to flick her gaze away. The yearning had been there, no matter how self-deluded the wish had been. The death of that hope twisted her lungs in her chest, filling her voice with the wretchedness that gripped her.

"But I expected you to care. Not a lot, but enough to keep me from dying in childbirth on the floor of our bedroom—" It wasn't even theirs anymore. It was hers.

Her throat seized and her eyes burned. She made herself fold the tiny jacket with trembling hands, refusing to look at him as she pushed her shattered expectations into an armored vault.

"Octavia." His voice sounded like she felt. Shocked and shredded and tight. Strong hands took her shoulders in a warm grasp as he turned her into him. "*I didn't know.*"

"You didn't want to know," she charged, knocking his hands away and stepping back. "You certainly never showed up to ask. He told me—" She didn't want to say it aloud, didn't want to know if it was true, but she had to face it if it was. "He said you were having affairs. Were you? Is that what happened? Are you in love with someone else?"

The look on his face created a kind of barometric pressure that couldn't be heard or seen, only felt, making the air go dense around her. Pulsing and thick.

"No," he said with understated thunder.

"I can't believe you could think for one *minute*—"

Octavia tensed at his incensed tone.

He cut himself off, doing everything he could to stay this side of civilized. It was a struggle. The picture she painted of her terror during labor, along with the accusation she was throwing at him like tar, clung and burned.

He was a man who took his responsibilities seriously, never behaved negligently, but he'd made a mistake. That was hard enough to take, but now this? Accusations of cheating?

"How would I know what you've been doing in Naples?" She was different. She'd hardened in the months since he'd seen her. As loving as she appeared toward Lorenzo, that was the only softness in her now as she stared at him, shades of denunciation and rejection skittering behind her eyes.

Something shook in his chest. Like a closed shutter taking a strong wind, testing the locks. It was painful. Disconcerting. Primo had been intent on hurting him. That was painful enough to face, but even more devastating was how effective Primo had been with his attack.

Octavia had been a delightfully easy addition to Alessandro's life, biddable and filled with a shy passion he had mined with a type of gold fever. He hadn't had to fight for her. Hadn't had to give up anything of himself to get what he wanted.

He had taken for granted that he had her. He could admit that he'd been arrogant on that front. But what the fallout from Primo's actions was rather graphically demonstrating was how nascent his connection to Octavia was. It was a piece of paper that bound their assets. He didn't have *her*.

That unsettled him, which was odd because he hadn't married for a love match. This, what they were enduring, was more angst than he had ever wanted to wade through. He'd deliberately sidestepped the highs and lows of an emotional landscape by marrying a woman who kept her own heart guarded.

Octavia pushing him away as she was doing, however, was the exact sort of chaos Primo had hoped to unleash.

"No one has ever accused me of so many dishonorable

things," he muttered. "But I am guilty of one thing only, Octavia, and that was trusting the wrong man."

Her mouth twitched before she firmed it into a stubborn line. There was something else in her demeanor, however. Something bleak. "I thought he might be lying, but…" She searched his eyes with indecision clouding her own.

The air thickened as he instinctively sensed something worse coming.

"He said you only got me pregnant for the bonus my father offered you. That you didn't care about how my pregnancy was going so long as Lorenzo delivered alive."

"Porco cane," he muttered, cursing his cousin while his mind exploded. "That is—" He had to move away and dig a hand into his hair. He clenched enough of a handful to hurt. *Dio*, at this rate his own security team would have to take him down if he was ever within five meters of his cousin. Otherwise he'd be jailed for first-degree murder.

"I was terrified for both of you," he said, voice hoarse as he revisited those hours between being informed that she needed emergency surgery and arriving to hear they'd come through safely. "He deliberately played with me, leaving me hanging with partial information. It was a nightmare."

She searched his expression and, just for a moment, he let the agony retake him. He let her see that he might not have been beside her, but he'd been with her.

But going to that place was dangerous. He couldn't control his reaction to having been sent there by someone he had thought he could trust. He slammed the door on that torment and looked away.

"He wanted to hurt us and we can't allow it. We can't let him destroy our marriage, Octavia. We can't let him win."

She swallowed, face pulling into lines of torture, chin dipping to hide her crumple of composure. She pulled a tissue from the box on the table. A tear fell as she quickly tried to swipe beneath her eyes. Her misery was a tangible thing he could taste on his tongue. An empathic sting in his throat and constriction in his chest gripped him, making breathing difficult.

He had to go to her, offer the comfort he should have given her all along. He pulled her into his lap as he sat on the sofa and *mio Dio* he wanted to kiss her so badly—

She stiffened as he gathered her so he only pressed his mouth to her temple, subtly drinking in her scent and parting his lips enough to taste her skin. She trembled and curled her fingers into his shirt, face tucking into his neck where he could feel the dampness of her cheeks against his throat.

She shuddered once, catching back a sob.

He cradled her closer, tighter, hoping the pound of his heart reached her. That she understood he wished he'd been here.

The separation of the past months had distanced them. They'd already been practicing abstinence as a precaution against miscarriage. Alessandro had fallen into a routine of working late then working out, blood afire in his veins, body craving hers like an addict withdrawing from drugs.

He'd borne it because he'd had to. Staying in Naples had made it easier, physically. Maybe a part of him had even wanted to prove he *could* stay away. Had it been ego-driven? He could still hear Primo's askance comment, *"You're going to fly all this way to cuddle her?"*

Now he wished he had. She was tense in his lap, accepting the embrace, but only marginally.

Rejection squeezed him in a dank hold. He ran the flat of his hand in a reassuring circle against her back, coaxing her to relax. Coaxing her to remember they'd had something. She could trust him.

"I was so scared," she whispered.

"I'm here now," he said, trying not to crush her, but he was anxious to imprint her with his presence.

She sniffed and her hand slid up, curling around his neck. Her torso angled so her breasts became a soft, erotic pressure against his chest. Her plump bottom was a sweet weight that shifted against an organ swelling and aching with pressure.

He started to seek her lips, hand shifting to the side of her face, but his mother's voice intruded from upstairs. She was looking for them. Dinner was ready.

"You need to eat," Alessandro said, heart racing as he snapped himself from a lascivious mind-set and loosened his hold, gently helping Octavia find her feet as he rose.

She clung for balance. The tightness of her shaking grip and the small flinch that arrived as she stood told him how sore she was at her incision. She released him quickly, folding the edges of her jacket across her breasts and hugging herself. She seemed very young in that moment and he reminded himself that she wasn't even twenty-four.

Seven years younger than him and not nearly so worldly. Hiding a lot. Why hadn't she called and shared her worries? What had that been about her father not caring about her best interests? How much had he missed by not being here?

She started toward the dining room and he urged her to pause with a touch on her arm. "Octavia. I should tell you, in case it comes up in future. Your father did offer me a bonus for a live birth. I found it…distasteful, to be honest. Hardly something within my control and not something I wanted a financial reward hanging upon. I told him to pay it out to you if he felt so strongly about it."

"He did," she said in a flat voice he found difficult to interpret. "It went into my account the other day and it is distasteful, but at least it gives me options."

CHAPTER SIX

ALESSANDRO WAS NEVER anything less than confident. Even when he'd been refusing to run the Ferrante corporate holdings there hadn't been any doubt in him over whether he could do it, only a firm belief he didn't deserve to. He certainly never backed down from a fight until he'd exhausted all his own options.

He wanted to leap on Octavia's comment, but now wasn't the time. She was emotionally exhausted and physically done in. He might not be as effusive as his mother, but they were both in agreement that Octavia needed rest and lots of it, so he didn't ask her to come to Paris with him, even though he wanted to.

He hated to leave her for even a minute, now that he realized how badly they'd fallen apart, but work needed piecing back together as much as his marriage.

Still, her remark continued to turn over in his mind, aggravating him even when he returned to his mother's house and found her napping. She was so different, so serious and perhaps even more reticent than when they'd first met.

By the end of their honeymoon, he'd been captivated by the woman he'd married. She'd been passionate as hell in bed, bright and funny yet thoughtful. There was no sign of that woman now and it was his fault.

He must have come across as smug in those early weeks,

because Primo had said, "*Lucky you*," with a sneer, and made a remark about how he would be happy to continue steering the ship if Alessandro wanted to go back to playing house.

Alessandro had seen the threat then, he acknowledged now, had even acted by sidelining his new wife in favor of asserting his position at work and within the family. He'd sent Primo to expand the London office and the confident woman who'd begun to blossom had soon been sent to the same cold climate where she'd been stepped on until she was completely closed against him.

He wanted their marriage back to where it had been last year, before he'd gotten her pregnant, when she'd been quick to come forward and kiss him in greeting, hands sliding around his waist as if she'd been waiting all day to touch him.

The way he had waited all day to hold her.

Instead, they were back to the very beginning. In the days leading up to their wedding, she had allowed his touch, but she'd been a lot like she was now: wary and unwilling to look him in the eye.

With a bittersweet smile, he recalled his gentle breaching of her defenses on their wedding night. She'd been apprehensive, but endearingly brave in her determination to overcome her qualms. He had enjoyed teasing her past her reservations one slow step at a time. Dancing to low, erotic music in their hotel room while she got used to the feel of his hands on her body. Undressing in the light of candle flame so her skin glowed as she blushed all over. He'd coaxed her to explore him and she'd reacted as though he was too hot to touch, hands drawn mothlike to his skin, then fluttering away.

He'd been the one to burn on contact. She'd been so responsive, moaning against his mouth and gasping as he circled her nipple with his thumb. When he'd pressed her to the bed and lightly explored her inner thighs, driving them both crazy with anticipation before he'd finally found what they were waiting for, she'd been wetly aroused, so slick and heated he nearly lost it just from exploring her.

"Do you do this to yourself? Show me what you like," he'd said, petting, enjoying the way she shivered and tensed and made strangled noises in her throat.

"I'm not going to tell you that," she'd choked, hand trembling over his as she tried to decide between the pleasure he was giving her and the bashfulness that was receding behind desire.

"You do," he'd teased, then commanded, *"Let me make it happen for you,"* and had tongued her nipple, sucking as he fondled her into climaxing with her hands in his hair and soft cries escaping her lips.

He had wanted to thrust into her then, so close to losing control he'd been shaking, but he'd gone down, arousing her all over again, carefully penetrating with his fingers to prepare her and making her arch up to his mouth as she gave up another orgasm.

Then, *then* he had covered her, gritting out, *"I'll be fast. It will only hurt for a minute."* He'd had nothing left for discipline and for the first time in his life he wasn't using a condom. But as he'd thrust into her, she had tensed in the wrong way, gasping an anxious, *"Wait."*

It had nearly killed him, but he'd kept himself still, eyes closed, breath held, racked in a state of exquisite torture. He'd been so aroused he had been one pulsing nerve that felt and smelled and heard. He had been completely in the moment, his entire world reduced to her silken clasp around him, her scent, her shaken breaths as she relaxed by slow degrees.

Finally, her soft lips had sought his, whispering a damp acquiescence against his mouth.

As he'd begun to move, he'd known what they were doing wasn't sex. It had been everything from the basest type of mating to the highest art form. He had promised to be fast, but he had wanted it to last his lifetime. His need to pour into her had been so acute he couldn't breathe. One more stroke, just one more then—

"Oh. I think I'm— Keep going. Don't stop. Please. Oh, oh."

Music and torment. He had guided her thigh to his waist and pushed a hand under her hip to angle her so he could drive deeper, kissing her hard as she dug her nails into his shoulders and sobbed with pleasure into his mouth. Then she had shuddered and rippled and had come again, pulling him with her so they were both tumbling through the same waves of mindless pleasure, clinging to each other while they drowned in ecstasy.

Alessandro came back to the quiet formality of his office in his mother's house and the patter of afternoon rain outside. He set a hand on the window, then his forehead, letting the cold of the pane penetrate, trying to take his hot blood down a few degrees.

He and Octavia were so damned attuned when they were having sex. It had only grown better from that first time and he was hard as a diamond just thinking about it. He wanted to cross the hall and slide into the bed where she was napping, and remind her exactly how well matched they were.

But seduction was off his playlist.

Wait. Was it? He ran a hand down his face, trying to pull himself together, thinking he didn't have to make love to her, just let her know he wanted to. Surely that would begin to reassure her?

A distant squawk told him his wife might not be awake, but his son was. He took custody of Lorenzo from the nanny, spending his first hour alone with the boy, fully taking in that he was a father now. That brought up memories of his own father and, if he had been looking for something to cool his ardor and shake him back to his priorities, there it was. He was glad of the privacy of his office as he dealt with the wrench of emotion.

Lorenzo was such an innocent. So perfectly unmarred by life. Alessandro enclosed the tiny boy in a protective cage against his chest, thinking how cavalier he'd been in producing this new life only so Lorenzo could struggle to hang on to it. This world was a harsh place. When he'd been making love to his wife, he hadn't taken in that he was increasing a thousandfold the level of responsibility he had carried since he was twelve years old. But now he had this small boy to guide and guard into manhood. Did Octavia really believe he would allow his child to grow up anywhere but under his own nose?

The magnitude of how completely his life had changed hit him. His cousin, the man he'd relied on, was gone. His wife wanted to leave him. He'd been given a son.

His entire path forward had to be reassessed, but he wouldn't move down it alone. Octavia was coming with him. That much he knew.

Octavia woke and went directly to her son, but he wasn't in his nursery. Ysabelle might have him downstairs, she supposed, but the door to the master suite was closed and…

She glanced at the door at the end of the hall. It was the office Alessandro used when he was here. He'd been in Paris all week, despite his assurance days ago that he was here now. The door to his office was almost always closed whether he was in there or not, but a sixth sense had her going to it and knocking.

"Alessandro?" She poked her head in.

He stood at his desk and looked up from reading something on his laptop screen, his expression of concentration clearing to distracted welcome. He was impeccable if casual with his jacket and tie gone, two buttons open and a baby in his crooked arm.

"You're up."

"You're home."

Apparently they were stating the obvious.

She suddenly realized her shirt collar was turned under, her hair loose and uncombed and her eyes still puffy with sleep. "I didn't know where he was. Is he hungry?"

"He hasn't said so," he said dryly, glancing at the blinking infant before inviting her in with a wave. He met her halfway into the room and let her take the baby. With a light touch against the side of her head, he held her for a brief but firm kiss, then moved past her to close the door. "How are you feeling?" he asked as he turned back to her.

"Good," she murmured, disconcerted by the faint taste of coffee now on her lips. "You're starting him rather early for taking charge, aren't you?"

"One more reason to raise him in Naples," he commented with quiet significance.

She looked away, but her gaze snagged on the oil painting by his aunt that hung behind his desk. It was the view from the veranda of the Castello di Ferrante onto the hills of the vineyard surrounding the ancestral estate.

"It's his heritage," Alessandro added, noting where she was looking.

As he said it, she heard the truth of it. She squirmed inwardly, but realized he had her. No matter what she thought best for herself, she couldn't deny Lorenzo his birthright.

Did Alessandro feel guilty at all using their son to manipulate her? If he did, there was not one iota of remorse in his expression.

"My grandfather used to tell me that being CEO of the family company is a caretaker's position. I thought I understood what he meant, but I didn't. Not until I brought my son in here today. I'm not just supporting the family, but building his future. You won't deny it to him, will you?"

Octavia let her gaze flicker around the room. The place was in disarray. Alessandro was obviously still trying to bring order after firing Primo. He'd left file cabinet drawers open and papers spilled onto every surface. An assortment of flash drives and backup tapes littered a side table and an old laptop had been revived on the coffee table. The desk was peppered with his own laptop and tablet and phone. One of Lorenzo's new stuffed bears sat crookedly in the big black executive chair like a tiny drunken CEO.

She didn't take in the mess so much as search for escape routes, glancing to the window like a bird seeking freedom. But the window was closed.

"No," she admitted in a small mumble of defeat. "Congratulations on finding my Achilles' heel." She glanced back at him, expecting triumph.

He was very somber. "My mother is going to sit with him tonight, so you and I can go out for dinner."

"Oh. I—" She hadn't expected that. After weeks of feeling too unwieldy to leave the house, then stuck in the hospital and finally recovering here, she was feeling very cooped up. The little bird in her gave a fresh flutter of its wings, but Ysabelle obviously didn't see the tension between her son and daughter-in-law. "That's a nice offer, but I'll tell her it's not necessary."

"I asked her to."

"Why?" she blurted.

"Because we've been apart too long. It's time to be a husband and wife again."

This was exactly what she was afraid of. The moment she conceded one point to him, he assumed she was ready to resume their marriage.

Was she?

She was still trying to decide a few hours later, as she applied makeup for the first time in forever. She was still attracted to her husband, of course she was. Physically, he was so perfect it was a superpower. But he was extra powerful in other ways, too, which made her feel weak.

She sighed, standing back to examine the top and skirt she'd rescued from her early maternity wear. The black skirt had a kerchief hem and an elastic panel that didn't put too much pressure on her abdomen. Her legs looked okay, especially once she stepped into a pair of heels. The overlong, eggplant-colored top was, well, she supposed the scoop neckline drew the eye to her cleavage, rather than the thick waistline she'd tried to define with a narrow gold belt. She looked voluptuous and very Italian, especially with her pregnancy hair, thick and wavy and longer than she'd ever worn it. With a quick twist, she wound a pale yellow-and-orange scarf around her neck, adding a hint of pizzazz.

"You look beautiful," he said, expression softening into admiring lines as he watched her come down the stairs to meet him in the foyer. He drew her close to press a kiss to her temple and her crumpled ego ate it up.

She tucked a mumbled, *"Grazie,"* into his shoulder. His touch took her tension into a whole new stratosphere, reminding her how much she enjoyed his caresses. At one point she'd been sure he enjoyed their lovemaking, too, but she wasn't so sure anymore.

She wasn't sure about anything, least of all why had she agreed to dinner.

As if he knew she was wavering, he kissed his mother, thanked her for babysitting and escorted Octavia out to the waiting car. Minutes later they were at the Mayfair restaurant she liked. It was converted from an eighteenth-century town house and she only visited for afternoon tea when she was on her own, but Alessandro had brought her here on the tail end of their honeymoon and she absolutely loved it. They always had excellent music, new art and the atmosphere was very trendy and creative, the food beyond exceptional.

He'd booked them a private table in the library and held her chair himself. She let him order, too busy looking at the sketches on the walls to read the menu herself. When the sommelier came, she murmured, "I'm not sure if I should have wine if I'm nursing."

"Water it down," Alessandro suggested, nearly making the sommelier drop the bottle that likely cost four figures.

"He's joking," Octavia assured the man, biting back a smile as she admonished Alessandro with a look, but she'd just glimpsed the playboy from her honeymoon and wanted to laugh with sheer and hopeful joy. "I'll have a very short glass and please don't be offended if I don't finish it."

When the man left, she told Alessandro, "That was mean," then clinked glasses with him. *"Salud."*

He lifted a negligent brow, settling back to regard her, fingers tracing the base of his glass where he set it on the table.

She sipped again. The wine was excellent. She'd have to be careful, nervous as she was. That would go down too easily if she let it.

"Where are your rings?" Alessandro asked, stilling.

He looked from her hand to her eyes, accusation sharp in his gaze.

"I took them off weeks ago because my hands were swelling. I can't get them back on yet." She tucked her hands into her lap.

"It's not symbolic then?" he asked, lifting his glass, but regarding her over the rim without tasting.

She parted her lips, but found too many words coming into her mouth, all jumbled and hard to speak. Meeting his gaze grew difficult and she dropped her attention to the middle of the table.

The silence grew heavy and loaded. "You were happy in our marriage, Octavia. You can be happy again."

Because he decreed it?

"It wasn't a marriage, Alessandro. It was an *affair*." Her voice thinned and her cheeks burned. It was hard to face the truth. Hard to speak it. "You took three weeks off work and I had a lover for the first time in my life. We did nothing but eat, swim and make love. Of course I was happy. But the minute we returned to reality, you set me aside."

The injury of that slow realization, as their sense of closeness was eroded daily by neglect, made her voice unsteady. "I wasn't sharing your life. I was the sex toy you took to bed at night."

His head went back. "That's insulting to both of us."

"You didn't have any use for me once we were told I couldn't have sex." She looked down at her hands knotting in her lap, peeled three fingers into a salute that she held up. "Three duty visits," she reminded him.

He looked away. His grip on the stem of his glass looked as if it would snap the delicate strand.

"Is it any wonder I believed Primo when he said you were cheating?" she added.

"I didn't even *think* of other women while we were

apart. I only want *you*," he said in a tone that fell somewhere between frustration and fury.

Yet, when he brought his attention back to her, his eyes glittered with banked lust. He looked at her like he had on their honeymoon. As if he'd battled his way past the guards and was opening the chest of booty.

Her heart stuttered in her chest. Her nerves tingled and the pit of her belly burned as though she'd swallowed half a bottle of gin. She held her breath, trying to withstand the huge rush of sexual excitement that suffused her.

"It's not like this for everyone, you know," he said. They were speaking Italian, were alone in the big room, but she blushed as he added, "You were a virgin, so you may not realize that, but we have something not everyone does, *cara*."

"The sex doesn't matter," she said, the color in her cheeks increasing under his incredulous stare. "It's not enough," she clarified, lifting a fatalistic hand, stammering out, "There has to be something else and obviously there isn't because nothing about me drew you here while I was pregnant. Not even your unborn son."

The remembered loneliness crept up to sting the backs of her eyes, making it hard for her to continue.

"How are we supposed to have any sort of marriage if you weren't interested in something as basic as friendship? If all you want from me is my body?" It absolutely crushed her to say it, but she had to face it. "I'm nothing to you. I can't be *nothing*, Alessandro."

"I regret not coming," he said, catching at her hand before she could tuck it back into her lap. His grip urged her to look at him. His dark brows formed a pained line over a gaze that reflected agony. "I will regret not being here for the rest of our lives because it might have prevented some of this…stage play we're barely surviving. You and

I would not be so far apart right now if I'd used that time to get to know you the way I should have.

"What can I say?" he continued, massaging her hands as though he wanted to work his words into her skin. "I'm arrogant. I believed we had the rest of our lives. Perhaps there was even some immaturity on my part, not quite ready to accept the yoke of marriage. My life has been one of autonomy. I wanted to be married, not domesticated. I'm not proud of that attitude, but I'm man enough to admit that's where my head was at."

"And now you're ready to be domestic?" she chided, letting her hand stay in his because she craved his touch. Even after all this time, all her anger and disappointment and reservations, she wanted to hold still for his touch.

"Now, like many people who only realize the true value of something when they almost lose it, I am ready to commit wholeheartedly to our marriage," he said in a tone that made it a vow.

Hope pulsed in her arteries. Everything about him weakened her: the control and confidence his posture projected, the handsomeness of his godlike features with that glint of determination in his eyes.

"But I can't say the same," she admitted, wavering slightly as he flinched and sent her a fierce look. "I went into this marriage so anxious for it to be perfect, so certain it would be better than my parents', I never disagreed with any of your decisions. You made all of them. I can't be that person you married. I won't."

"I'm not asking you to," he said, holding her hand a little tighter as a more avid light came into his eyes, like a hunter pouncing on its prey. "But does your first demand of me have to be that I allow you to leave me and take our son? That's unreasonable. Try again."

She released a husk of a disbelieving laugh, sitting back

and stealing her hand away from his. "I suppose asking you to quit being so arrogant is also unreasonable?"

"And unrealistic," he said without a hint of sheepishness or apology. "I don't compromise, Octavia. That's not who I am, but I'm trying to do it for you," he added sincerely. "For my wife. To save our marriage. Do you see that?"

She swallowed, weirdly affected by that statement. A sip of wine was in order, to help her digest everything he'd said. Warmth ran down her limbs.

"Believe it or not, I don't want a spineless wife," he said. "Yes-men annoy me. That's why I'm furious to learn that all this time, when I thought you were content, you've been miserable and keeping it from me."

She bit the insides of her lips before she said simply, "It never mattered to anyone how I felt. My parents didn't care and boarding school—" She shrugged that off. No welcome for whiners there.

Their *feuilletés* arrived, distracting them for a moment as they broke the delicate puff pastries. They were tiny, only two bites, and shaped like fish. Creamy salmon and asparagus filling oozed out.

"Tell me more about your parents. You said a few days ago that your father didn't have your best interests at heart, but he was very shrewd in our meetings. He wanted a good marriage for you."

She dipped her chin, reproving him for thinking her father's demands had had anything to do with her. "If you are a caretaker of your family fortune, he is a hoarder, one who is frustrated that he can't take his money with him. He wanted a successor and got a vessel. I told you about my mother's miscarriages. I didn't fully appreciate how horrible that must have been for her until now, when I have my own baby, but I've always felt…" She shrugged. "Obligated to do what they wanted, otherwise why did she go through all that to have me? But given her delicate pregnancies and bouts of depression when she lost them... I assume she went through spells of refusing to sleep with my father and so he cheated. It didn't make for a very happy home to grow up in."

Her fork went under the last minuscule bite of the delicious starter. As she swallowed, she looked up to see him watching her. Was that compassion in his gaze? Concern?

"Please don't pity me. It is what it is."

He drew a breath and stood, coming to her side where he held out a hand.

"What—?" She looked up, up, up to muscled shoulders straining the pin-striped fabric of his shirt. His stance was one of invitation, not intimidation, but her heart still skipped in alarm. She caught the faint scent of the aftershave he'd applied this morning. Its spicy fragrance was overlain with the more simple, masculine fragrance of him, heady and drugging.

"The music has started. Let's dance."

"I— Here?" She glanced around at the room containing a handful of empty tables, sparks of light glancing off the glass of the framed sketches. "There's not a lot of room."

"We don't need a lot of room. I'm going to hold you very close."

Little shivers went through her as he picked up her hand and she found herself standing, letting him draw her to him. He'd done this before, on their honeymoon, when she'd been so apprehensive about their wedding night she had bordered on telling him to "just get it over with."

He had done this, though. Held her. Soothed her. His touch was light, yet confident. He was warm and strong, his arms a place of safety while the brush of their bodies revealed he was aroused.

She wanted to weep with relief that she could still affect him, but anxiety struck at the same time. "You know I can't—"

"I know. I still want to hold you," he murmured, lips brushing her brow. "I wish you'd told me about your parents before. You want a better life for Lorenzo, don't you? We can have one, Octavia. I promise you we can. Give our marriage another try," he coaxed, more gentle than dictatorial, but it was a command, not a request. "We'll both give it a proper try."

Oh, he was smooth, lulling her with the lazy circles of his palm on her back.

"I suppose I should take heart from the fact you're saying that even though we can't sleep together," she muttered, turning her curled fingers on his chest to look at her fingernails.

"We'll sleep together, *cara*." He stopped swaying and tilted up her chin. His strong thumb caressed her skin while he lightly cupped her throat in his wide hand.

She instinctively turned her hand on his chest to press, staying him from making an advance.

Their gazes locked.

He must have felt the way her pulse was kicking. Beneath her palm, she was surprised to feel his heart punching with similar ferocity, making her tingle all over, as if they were caught in a force field that held them joined and motionless, frozen with anticipation.

He was going to kiss her.

"Do you want to?" he asked in a graveled tone. He wasn't asking about a kiss. He was asking if she wanted to sleep with him.

She wished she could look away from his gray-green eyes. "I just told you I can't," she reminded him.

A very faint smile tilted his mouth. "That's not what I asked."

And she was transported back to the first time he had kissed her. After spending two hours locked in her father's office, days after their first meeting at the gala, he had left the room and his tracking gaze had found her and locked in. He'd come across to put a ring on her finger and asked, *"Shall we seal the deal?"*

She'd already been nervous while he spoke to her father, then terrified as she realized what he meant. It hadn't been her first kiss, but it had certainly been the first one she'd felt like pure spirits burning down her middle. Heat had poured across her skin and made her fingers and toes tingle. She'd opened her mouth instinctively, accepting the exploration of his tongue. She'd loved it.

A thousand kisses had followed, all of them exquisitely delicious. She loved kissing him. Nothing compared.

But if she kissed him now, it would imply agreement.

Doubts continued to float and burst like rainbow-colored bubbles around her, but her gaze dropped to his mouth. She was giving in. She could feel herself surrendering the fight...

Because she really, really wanted him to kiss her.

His head lowered.

She expected a crush of ownership. Triumph even.

He kissed her like he had that first time. Lightly. Sweetly. Gradually coaxing her to part her lips and let the heat and dampness spread.

She was the one who slid her arms around his neck and leaned in and encouraged him to increase the pressure. She opened her mouth and fisted her hand in his hair and punished him for making her wait so long to feel alive. She had missed the sexual energy, the rush of excitement, the provocative differences in their bodies that stimulated her in ways she couldn't even explain. She kissed him hard and drove her tongue into his mouth and made a noise of anger and relief.

He locked hard arms around her, holding her tight, just short of squeezing her. His hands moved with possessive familiarity, one splaying under her bottom and angling her hips into his groin.

She rubbed against him, inciting him with the grind of her hips and the scrape of her teeth against his lips. She wanted to bite him. Hurt him.

He grunted, kissing her harder as he took control, holding her with restrained power just short of crushing her while he pulled at her lips and ravaged her mouth.

To hell with her recovery and the tenderness across her belly. *She wanted him.* Her body went weak, signaling her willingness to be taken.

She felt the reaction in him, the gather of his muscles as if he would pick her up and carry her to the nearest surface. The floor. He had in the past.

He tore his mouth from hers instead, one hand moving to the back of her head to tuck her crown under his chin where he held her as though protecting her from the fireball that had exploded into flames between them. They panted, hearts slamming.

To her eternal shock, she realized they were in a restaurant. Voices drifted over the music from the other rooms.

She closed her eyes, needing this moment to collect herself. That had been raw and voracious. Alarming. They'd never been like that before. It made her a little frightened for when they *could* make love again. They might shred each other to pieces.

"It hurts," he said gruffly. The hand low on her spine pressed just enough to make her aware of the iron-hard muscle digging into her tender abdomen. "It hurts to touch you and not have you. To smell your hair and feel you against me and kiss without having the rest. It damned well *hurts*, Octavia. That's why I stayed away. But I'm not letting you leave me."

Fine trembles gripped her as she tried to think and couldn't. She just wanted to feel. She wanted him. She wanted to believe this was something they could build on.

"You haven't even said you're sorry," she managed to say, forcing herself to pull back enough to see him. Pathetic as she was, she needed his support to stand, even as her voice cracked with suffering.

Remorse convulsed his features.

"I am sorry." It wasn't an apology. He wasn't trying to convince her. It was a statement. "Deeply sorry. I took you for granted and underestimated my cousin. But how can I ask your forgiveness when I'll never forgive myself?"

She'd never heard that particular scrape in his voice before. Never seen such a bleak, devastating anguish leech out all the green to completely gray his eyes. His fingers on her arms were gentle, but she felt pain from them. *His* pain.

An urge to comfort pressed her heart toward him, giving her a flat, aching sensation against the inner wall of her chest. She wanted to tell him it was all right, but it wasn't. And he knew it. He felt it. He wasn't as oblivious as she feared, which filled her with that wretched, misguided hope that kept sparkling before her like a lure.

He very tenderly caressed her cheek, fingertips smoothing her hair back and tracing a line down her jaw. The backs of his knuckles grazed under her chin and down the delicate, pulsing cords in her throat.

"We'll save sleeping together for when we reach Italy. I want you to rest as much as you can while we're here. Heal." His touch, the look in his eyes, made it sound as though he wanted more than physical repair for her.

As though he understood her heart was fractured and needed time.

The first tendrils of mending began as she glimpsed the man who'd turned her inside out on a three-week honeymoon, concerned and focused and with a touch like magic, thumb grazing her bottom lip so it felt puffy and incapable of anything but kissing.

Their next course came, but they just stood there, looking into each other's eyes. After a long moment, he dropped one more very, very gentle kiss on her mouth and slowly released her, leaving her burning as he drew her back to their table.

CHAPTER SEVEN

SHE WENT TO Naples with him. They landed three weeks later and went straight to see his grandfather at the Castello di Ferrante.

The *castello* would be Alessandro's one day, but all of his extended family came and went, treating it as a hotel. A few members were more or less permanent, something Octavia privately viewed as squatting. Alessandro's youngest sister had been one of them until recently, before her modeling career took off. Now she might have a room here, but she spent most of her time in Milan, Paris and New York.

From the few times they'd spoken, Octavia had liked all of her husband's sisters, but the older two had families of their own and lived in other parts of the country so she didn't see them often. Alessandro had far more cousins than she did and was close with many of them. It was an odd dynamic for her to have been thrust into since most of her father's siblings had emigrated to America and Australia before she was born and her mother was standoffish with her side. Octavia had grown up in a familial void made worse by being an only child. It had made her feel like an anomaly in her own country, where big dinners and frequent reunions were the norm.

She'd always wanted to feel a part of a warm, gregarious family and suspected she would turn into the clichéd

Italian mother doting on her son into his forties, but for now she was still daunted by the many-stranded web of Alessandro's blood ties.

And she had never been able to see herself as the matriarch of that network and this house. Whenever she came here to the *castello*, she felt like a very temporary, barely tolerated guest.

She loved the place all the same.

As they began the climb that wound through the lower portion of the vineyard, she took in the beauty of the estate. Even in winter it was covered in the lush confusion of the estate manager's intensive farming techniques. With the land so fertile, Alessandro's grandfather put every speck of dirt to work. Olive trees bordered the rows of grapes. Beneath the orange trees, the lavender had been cut back for winter. Garlic and runner beans would soon spring up in the lemon grove. Strawberries, their leaves faded by winter, surrounded the fig trees and the stacked plots where the tomatoes and basil would grow were freshly turned and ready.

Then the house rose to its full glory. Its yellow stone and red-tiled roof held a matte finish in the weak sunlight, but its sprawling wings and elegant balconies were as aristocratic as ever. It was gracefully aged, never old.

The driver pulled the SUV to a stop in a crunch of gravel between the fountain and the wide front steps. They were keeping the protection of a security team as a precaution, but Bree was quick to leap from the front seat and scan the layered balconies and small terraces across the upper levels of the *castello*. She was only four years younger than Octavia, but made her feel ancient.

Octavia bumped knuckles with Alessandro as they both tried to release the baby from the straps of his car seat.

"I'll do it," Alessandro said, but caught her hand. "Rings still don't fit?"

"I didn't try them this morning. Too tired," she said truthfully, disturbed as he gave her fingers a gentle massage, trickling warmth through her.

She knew what he was doing with all these seemingly absent caresses; he'd done the same thing in the weeks leading up to their wedding night. It was a type of calculated seduction and she wished she didn't respond to it, but she did. He was gorgeous in a three-piece suit and tie, while she felt dowdy in a wrap dress and low heels, her makeup applied hastily on the plane to try to disguise the circles under her eyes.

"Things will be calmer now we're home," he promised.

Except they weren't home. They were staying here at the *castello*, through his grandfather's birthday, before they would finally return to the town house in a week or so to properly start their life afresh.

She wished she had as much confidence in their marriage now as she'd had going into it nearly a year ago. Ignorance was bliss, she supposed, because today she held a lot of trepidation for the gauntlet that had to be endured here and the return to the life she'd failed to master the first time around.

But Alessandro meant that being away from his mother would be more peaceful.

Octavia missed her already and hadn't wanted to leave London, but Ysabelle had been leaving to see her count anyway. Besides, every time Octavia had decided she didn't want to come to Italy with Alessandro, he'd done something considerate like take Lorenzo when he was fussing or brought her something to eat or drink when she sat down to nurse. It had been a lot easier to resent him when they'd been apart. When he was near, handsome and attentive, dropping little kisses and caresses on her, she slipped back into blind adoration.

More important, even though he happily handed off diaper duty to the nanny, she had observed him showing a sincere attachment to their son. This morning she'd overheard their man-to-man chat about world markets and which investments to avoid for the next year. It amused her all over again thinking of it. He'd sounded so serious, asking Lorenzo for his opinion on the matter.

So there was one fact she couldn't deny in all of this: Lorenzo deserved to have his father in his life.

Which meant she had to find her place in Alessandro's.

No matter how daunting the prospect.

She drew a long, subtle breath as the *maggiordomo* came out the open doors of the *castello* and down the stairs. He greeted her with one of his polite nods. "The family is eager to meet the new arrival, Signora. They're waiting in the front parlor."

Wonderful. Octavia found a smile.

Alessandro came around the car with Lorenzo bundled in one arm. He held out his free hand to her, sparing a moment to offer her a steady look. Gratitude? Pride? She wasn't sure how to interpret it.

She swallowed, unsteady as they climbed the stairs and entered together.

The first time they'd come here, fresh off their honeymoon, Primo's sister had taunted Alessandro for not carrying her over the threshold. Alessandro had dismissed the remark, stating it was his grandfather's house and not appropriate.

Octavia hadn't said anything, but Alessandro hadn't performed the whimsical ceremony at the town house, either, and his overlooking of the gesture had felt like a put-down. It had been the first hard landing into reality after the giddy spell of lovemaking and basking in his attention. She'd never been able to walk through this door without thinking of his dismissive tone and how harshly it reminded her that their marriage was a business transaction, not something based on sentiment or affection.

And here she was again. Not Octavia, the woman he loved and carried into his family home, but the consigned wife he'd pressured to accompany him. If that wasn't lukewarm enough, she nearly caught frostbite from the group that greeted them. She nervously scanned the faces, so many of them Primo's closest relations, including Primo's parents.

Was it paranoid, now that Primo's subterfuges were exposed, to see all this occupancy of the *castello* in a new light? She took a half step closer to her husband, disturbed.

One of Alessandro's spinster aunts, a flighty wisp of a woman who preferred her paints over just about anything else and usually took no interest in enigmatic things like children, was the first to speak.

"Handsome. Like his father," she pronounced after a brief look at Lorenzo.

Primo's eldest sister, Donna, who had moved in with her teenage son last year said, "Don't be too sure, *Zia*. Perhaps this baby mix-up was an attempt to hide the fact neither of the infants are Ferrantes. Did you think of that, Sandro?"

Barely a minute in and the claws were out. Of course, it was to be expected that Primo's parents and sisters would defend their kin, but Octavia was struck by the open enmity in her remark. She and Donna might not have been friends, but they hadn't been adversaries. She pressed even closer to her husband and felt his grip on her hand tighten.

"He's ours," Alessandro confirmed, low and sure, practically daring anyone to contradict him.

"Bring him to me," Ermanno Ferrante said with an imperious wave of his hand.

He wasn't a tall man. His children and grandchildren towered over him, but he was still spry and sharp-eyed despite his weathered skin and steel-gray hair. He sat with the arrogantly regal posture that Alessandro must have learned from him, because they both had the ability to command a room with a look.

Alessandro tugged Octavia with him as he carried Lorenzo across. She could feel Ermanno's gaze drilling into her as she approached. He was capable of the same force and power that Alessandro possessed, but what was he looking for? Artifice? Proof? Guilt?

"Nonno, your great-grandson Lorenzo," Alessandro said, leaning down to kiss his grandfather and set the baby in the old man's arms.

Octavia would have kissed him in greeting, too, but the old man bent his head to give the baby a long, thorough study.

Behind her, she heard a few feet shuffle as everyone awaited his judgment.

"He looks like your father," he said with a glance up to Alessandro. Then he nodded his head toward the side table. "Bring the photo."

Octavia's knees nearly gave in as she moved to fetch the black-and-white of Alessandro's grandmother holding her firstborn and she had to agree, there was a strong similarity in the babies' sleeping features. It was bittersweet to see the resemblance, making her see her son's place in this family while reinforcing that she couldn't take him away from it.

"You'll understand if we're not happy," Viviana, Primo's youngest sister, said.

"Babies make everyone happy." Alessandro pivoted,

voice light with contradiction, but his tone held an edge that put a knot in Octavia's stomach.

"We're not happy with the things you've done, Sandro," Viviana clarified, chin coming up in belligerence.

"I've done exactly what I'm supposed to do—react to threats and limit damage," he said without apology. "Nonno, Octavia and the baby need to rest. I'll settle them in our apartment, then we can talk in the office. *Zio,* you may join us if you like. I imagine you have a few questions."

Primo's father, Giacomo, made a noise as if he had a lot more than a *few* questions about his son being arrested and fired and expelled from the family residences. Octavia felt the blister of hostility off everyone in the room, much of it aimed at her.

So she bit back saying that she wasn't *that* tired. The past few nights had been rough ones sleepwise, but her incision was itchy rather than tender and physically she was starting to feel like her old self.

But this was too awful to endure. She let Alessandro take her up to the suite they always used. He went through to the sitting room where a temporary nursery had been arranged. Bree took Lorenzo and Alessandro came back to their bedroom, closing the door behind him.

"I want to go to the town house," Octavia said firmly. There was no way she could sleep here. The verdant estate was beautiful and the view gave way to a distant scape of the city against the smudged blue of the bay, but antagonistic waves penetrated the walls and floors.

"Putting off this confrontation will only make it worse." He unbent her folded arms and stole her light coat, tossing it to a chair and nudging her toward the bed. "But can you see that if I had left you in London, they would have held you in suspicion? By bringing you back to face them, you're showing them you're blameless." He pressed her shoulder to sit on the edge of the bed, then he bent to pick up her feet, tipping her onto her side while he removed her shoes. "Once I make it clear that *I* fired Primo and the hospital is pressing charges, as well, they won't hold you accountable."

"I've never known you to be delusional, Sandro," she said on a dry laugh. "If they didn't warm up to me in the past, they certainly won't now."

He paused in reaching for the blanket folded on the foot of the bed.

"What did you say?"

"That you're being optimistic. If it was just me, I could take their dislike, but I'm scared for Lorenzo. I realize he doesn't even know what he's in the middle of, but—"

"This is *for* Lorenzo, but no. What did you call me?" He dropped the blanket and sat his hip next to hers on the mattress.

His weight rolled her into him and a funny self-consciousness washed over her. "They all call you Sandro. I didn't think you minded if I did."

"You haven't called me that in months." His hand went to the outside of her thigh, light but familiar, making tingles fan out from the spot across her abdomen and down to her knee and inward to her loins.

She shifted, but he didn't let the movement dislodge his hand.

"I didn't notice," she murmured. Avoiding his nickname hadn't been a conscious decision and she couldn't believe it mattered to him either way. The fact that he was remarking on it now made her use of the familiarity seem overly significant and intimate. She looked away, gaze scanning the ceiling for somewhere safe to land, but he lifted his hand off her hip and touched her chin, drawing her to look back at him.

The moment grew even more momentous for no reason at all. Neither of them spoke, but it was as if she'd opened a door and a million emotions had flooded in.

He was coming into her. And he took up a lot of space.

She desperately wished she could backpedal, but she couldn't. All she could do was close her eyes in an attempt to shut him out. "I am tired," she lied.

The mattress shifted and his breath warmed her lips before he kissed her.

She almost lifted a hand, wanting to draw it out. Her lips clung, but he kept the contact brief.

"We will get through this, *cara*," he said, making it sound like a vow.

He stood and opened the blanket across her, letting it drift down in a puff of air and a layer of softness and warmth.

As he left, she kept her stinging eyes closed tight and tried to believe he wasn't being optimistic. She wanted so badly to believe him.

But what if he was wrong?

Alessandro reentered the suite an hour later and saw the bed was empty. Clothes were strewn on the chair and the foot of the mattress. She wasn't in the bathroom.

He was so keyed up, his heart lurched in his chest, convinced in that first second that she'd left in a hurry, but her cases were still here, one of them open on the floor near the closet.

The door into the sitting room was also open. He strode in to find Lorenzo asleep, which was reassuring, but there was no sign of the nanny or Octavia.

A hand appeared on the brocade curtain and Octavia

peered at him from where she was sitting in the sun on the balcony. "Are you hungry? I ordered for both of us."

He stepped outside to join her, finding her picking over a selection of antipasto, the scene so commonplace it made his leap to wrong conclusions embarrassing.

"I came up to see if you were awake and wanted to join us for a late lunch." He stole a square of sharp cheese and hunger contracted his stomach. He dug in to the rest. "Where's Bree?"

"I said I'd listen for Lorenzo so she could introduce herself to the kitchen and walk the grounds, get her bearings. Don't eat all the olives."

His mouth twitched at her command, still not used to her new assertiveness, but there was something engaging about it. Like finding unexpected talent in your tennis opponent so the match was more challenging.

He was about done with challenges for the moment, though, he thought with a scowl.

He slid his attention to the tomato slices sprinkled with chopped basil and scooped a circle of toasted bread into the tapenade, topped it with an artichoke heart, then chased it with two of the stuffed grape leaves.

"You could have brought him down," he chided. "You're hiding." Not that he blamed her. He had no desire to go to the dining room now he was here.

"I'm acclimating," she corrected. "It's nice to feel the sun and smell the earth and hear Italian again." She tilted her closed eyes to the sky.

His conscience pinched, but then he reminded himself she'd been considering staying in London. He might have sent her away, but he'd brought her home, too.

The thought didn't ease the havoc inside him. His muscles were still twitching with aggression after holding himself back so heroically in his meeting with his grandfather and his uncle.

A fierce need to see his wife had driven him in swift steps up to their room. Funny how, after years of being the safety net for his entire family, he'd alienated nearly all of them and really only had an ally in Octavia. No one else appreciated the depth of betrayal he was experiencing and it bound him to her in a way he hadn't recognized until his uncle had confronted him on it.

"What hold does she have on you that you'd choose her over Primo?" That bark from Giacomo had lit a fire in Alessandro. His own grandfather had asked if there was some way—or reason—her family could have done this.

Octavia was his *wife*, he'd near shouted in completely uncharacteristic ferocity. They'd stared at him flatly. The statement wasn't an explanation.

You don't choose a woman over your family, his uncle had spat, adding to his grandfather, *He was always unpredictable.* It had been a deliberate attempt to goad Alessandro into losing his temper completely.

It had nearly worked. Instead, he'd said something that he hadn't even computed until the words had come out of his mouth. *"Octavia is my family. She and my son are as much my family as any of you. I protect all of my family. Provided they remain loyal to me."*

Thankfully Octavia's eyes remained closed and she couldn't see the barely banked rage he was still struggling to contain. Or his confusion as he belatedly wondered if he really was choosing his marriage over his fealty to the Ferrantes. He had fashioned himself into a bastion of dependability and allegiance and *couldn't* let a woman shake his resolve. That's why he hadn't wanted a love match when he married.

But as she'd held him off this past month, showing more

caution than warmth, he'd been acutely aware of a sense of loss. He was ready to do just about anything to get back what he'd had.

Which disturbed him.

Leaning his backside on the balcony rail, he studied his wife, trying to determine how she was managing to affect him so deeply. She wasn't a calculating femme fatale making a deliberate effort to provoke him. Quite the opposite. In some ways she was more aloof than when they'd first met, but wasn't doing it as a lure.

She was genuinely disappointed and mistrustful, which cut a straight line through his ego.

Plus, she was so beautiful his throat hurt just looking at her. The baby weight still softening her pretty features made them even more sensual and fascinating. Her hair was loose and longer than he remembered it. He wanted to comb his hands through the silky strands, letting them caress between his fingers, then bury his nose in the almond-and-nutmeg scent. That hair of hers had been a fetish since his first whiff. Why?

Her color was better, he noted, though her brow remained tense and there was an underlying anxiety in the somberness of her mouth. She still seemed very wary and worried.

But she'd called him Sandro earlier. It had been so sweet it had touched off a pang in his chest, until he'd seen how badly she'd wanted to swallow it back, fearful she'd let her defenses down too far. He'd taken such encouragement from that little slip and had been shaken by how much she'd regretted letting it happen.

He sighed at the gridlock before him.

She opened her eyes.

"Don't you want to look at the view?" She indicated the

cushioned chair on the other side of the table, then nodded past him to the sweep of land toward the distant water.

"I am," he said, delivering his compliment with a dose of self-mockery, mostly because it was so damned true. He could barely take his eyes off her.

And he wasn't above using every weapon at his disposal to overcome her defenses, even flattery.

Which he supposed she realized because she dismissed his words with a downward sweep of her lashes. It should have been a relief that she didn't know how sincere he was in his praise of her, that he was entranced by her, but it just reminded him that she didn't even trust him to be honest about something as simple as her beauty.

The food he'd eaten grew heavy as gravel in the pit of his gut.

After a moment, she lifted her attention to him, her expression grave. "How did it go?"

He shrugged shoulders that were prickling from the penetrating heat of the sun, instinctively wanting to shut down a rehash of what had been a very difficult conversation. But his efforts to protect her had backfired in the past. He supposed she had a right to know what they were up against.

"My grandfather is understandably troubled. Giacomo is livid."

She glanced back toward where Lorenzo slept, brow knitting with consternation.

"No, *cara*," he reassured in a quick hush, stepping forward. He leaned down to kiss the part in her hair, surreptitiously stealing a caress and inhaling her scent, but trying to impart comfort, too. He was a physical man and found it easier to show than to tell, but he did his best to assuage her fears with words, too. "He won't harm him. And I won't let anyone try."

"You're sure?" She caught his hand.

Her fingers were cold and the tightness with which she clung was both heartening and worrisome. He liked that she was looking to him and seemed so willing to take his word. It was a first step in rebuilding her belief in him, but it made him realize how frightened she was under her composed exterior. He was learning that his wife was a woman of far more complexity than he'd given her credit for.

Which was a concern on many levels, but for now he had to alleviate her fear.

He hooked his foot around the leg of the empty chair and dragged it around so he faced her, not letting go of her hand. He spoke in an undertone that wouldn't carry to open windows or below to the gardens.

"I am sure, but we are facing a greater battle than I anticipated. Primo wasn't the only one playing politics or resenting my position."

"I never thought it significant before," she murmured. "Until we arrived today and I saw that almost everyone who lives here… They're all Giacomo's children. There's your aunt, but she travels so much this isn't really where she lives, is it? And no one from your father's or his sister's side."

They'd all had seemingly valid reasons for moving in and it was his grandfather's house. Alessandro hadn't considered it an appropriation, especially when his grandfather was in fine health and Alessandro preferred his town house because it was closer to work. Through Octavia's eyes, however, he saw things much differently.

Especially after today's conversation.

"My uncle is trying to convince my grandfather to let him have control again. So I may have an opportunity to put my house in order." Disdain curled his lip as he recalled the suggestion. "I said he has some work to do in his own.

I *am* in control, legally, so it's not within my grandfather's rights to remove me, but I didn't want to insult him by reminding Giacomo of that in front of him. Things will get uglier before they settle into place."

The wrinkle in her brow deepened. "When I went off to school, there was a girl in her last year there. Her father had a bone to pick with mine. To this day, I don't even know what the problem was, but she turned me into persona non grata. I feel like that's how it's going to be here."

She was pale and, despite the new mettle she was showing toward him, very sensitive. He saw it now, underneath the impassive expression she'd no doubt perfected against cold shoulders.

A weight settled on his heart, an apology on his lips.

"I'm asking a lot, I know." He massaged her hand, still bare of his rings. Even though he knew she wasn't leaving them off to hurt him, he disliked how her empty fingers suggested their marriage had been set on a windowsill to collect dust. He wanted the statement of their commitment back where it was prominent and visible.

But the rings were the least of his problems. He forced himself to maintain a light hold on her fingers, even though a subversive sense of urgency made him want to close his grip and hang on tight. Was he harming her—*them*—by insisting she face this with him? When she'd already been through so much and confrontation wasn't her strong suit?

Was it even necessary for her to be here? After his uncle's questioning of his loyalty, he had to wonder if these final weeks of restructuring might be easier if Octavia wasn't under everyone's noses.

Even as he considered sending her away, he rejected the idea. He wasn't giving her up. Not when it was exactly the result Primo had hoped for.

Octavia had been a source of tension in the family from

the moment he had married her, he saw now. His taking a wife and producing an heir was the assertion of his position as overseer of the Ferrante empire. Apparently Primo hadn't been the only one to find that threatening. From his Uncle Giacomo through that branch of the family, there was disapproval and antagonism.

The opposition Sandro had only subconsciously acknowledged in his cousin last year was flagrant now. Leaving Octavia in London had given them all breathing space, but it had been a mistake. Sandro wouldn't abandon her again and it was a decision that had less to do with defending his right to his heritage and more to do with how precarious his marriage was. If Giacomo and the rest of the family made these next few weeks difficult enough, he could lose Octavia and he simply refused to.

For the millionth time in the past four weeks, he wished he could sweep her into their bed, make love to her and reforge the connection they needed. Instead, he had to watch her fingers twitch nervously under his touch and her bottom lip catch between her teeth.

How did one earn a woman's trust if not by demonstrating that even though he was strong enough to overpower her, he would only ever use his agility and strength to pleasure and protect her?

"What happened when your father died?" she asked, unexpectedly shaking him out of his rumination. "Did your uncle not challenge your right to command then?"

The memory of that dark time rose quick and fast to strike his heart like a rusted iron blade. He sat back, dropping her hand and trying to close the topic as swiftly and bluntly as he could.

"He didn't have to. He was put in charge as a provision in the directorship. I was too young and too trapped in grief to properly take in the politics or legalities. Plus, I felt so guilty I refused to even train for the position, so he dismissed me as a threat. It was years before I considered it, even longer before I was ready to usurp him."

He cut himself off as he realized he'd said too much.

Octavia cocked her head in curiosity. "What do you mean you refused? Why did you feel guilty?"

He didn't want to talk about it. He couldn't revisit the past without self-hatred overtaking him. His grandfather was the one who had insisted he assume the role, pushing and testing and guiding, telling him he owed it to his father to care and provide for the family the way his father would have done if he'd lived.

Alessandro flinched as his crisis of faith crept up to revisit him.

In light of all they were going through, did he deserve to oversee the family fortune? Had he caused this fissure in the family by marrying her instead of allowing Primo to do it?

How would Octavia see his actions? Would she side with his grandfather's view that he owed it to his father to shoulder the responsibility? Or with his own view that he was unworthy? Or with Giacomo's dismissal that he was unpredictable.

Unfit.

"We were at a festival," he said, rubbing suddenly chilly hands on his thighs. He cleared the huskiness from his voice. "I was twelve. You know that. I had a fight. It was a stupid argument between a pair of boys wanting to test each other. You understand what I mean? Hormones and immaturity. Bravado. Nothing more. But it felt like everything at the time."

That was always the part that bothered him most: how quickly his fuse had lit and how blindly he'd acted.

"I didn't even know him," he said, berating himself all

over again as he went back to that day, with its smell of dust and the heat off the buildings and sidewalks, even though the sun was down. The jarring music, the din of the crowd, the aroma of cooking thick on the air, it was all imprinted on him. "I took offense to something he said about my sister and stood up for her. We began to scrap. There would have been no harm beyond a pair of bloody noses. There were police there to keep the peace and one blew his whistle. That made my father look up from across the street. He was with some friends and had had a few drinks. He wasn't drunk, just tipsy enough to react without thinking. He stepped off the sidewalk to come across and stop me, but he didn't look. A car hit him and he was killed instantly."

"Oh, Sandro," she gasped, hand coming up to cover her mouth, as shocked as the entire street had been with the abruptness of it.

Her eyes held deep compassion, which wasn't easy to bear when he expected, even wanted, recrimination. But he'd traveled this road many times with his grandfather. He had come to terms with his guilt.

Mostly.

He stood, restless, trying to shake off the darkness.

Sandro moved into the sitting room and stood over the boy who carried his father's blood as well as his name.

Octavia gave him a moment as she took stock herself. Her husband was such a confident man. She never would have guessed he carried such a terrible burden on his conscience.

Following him, she saw the sun was beginning to angle across to Lorenzo's cot. She closed the doors and curtains, dimming the room.

"Is that why your uncle continues to challenge you?"

she asked gently. "He holds you responsible for his brother's death?"

Sandro jerked, then nodded once, keeping his back to her as he stared at their son. "Yes. And it's why Primo felt he had a right to this role."

"But he's not…" *you*, she wanted to say.

He lifted his head, seeming to hang on to what she'd been about to say.

"They're not like you," she said awkwardly. "Primo is selfish and Giacomo doesn't have your patience. There's no one else in the family…like you." She wasn't expressing herself well at all, but how did she describe his calm acceptance of responsibility, as if million-dollar decisions were nothing more than a choice between coffee or tea? He sifted through a hundred details and distilled a problem and found the solution all within seconds.

His reaction was difficult to read. His head went back a little as he absorbed her summation of his relatives, making her wonder if she'd crossed a line. Dismay curled his lip before he sighed.

"At any other time I would have defended them, but you're right. I've never wanted to see it, but of course you have." He looked at her as though reassessing her. "You keep your opinions to yourself, but you gather a lot, don't you? You're very astute." He pushed his hands in his pockets, shoulders tense. "But if you think me selfless and patient, it's because my grandfather taught me to be everything this family needs, so I could provide what my father would have given if he'd lived. I've let my guilt blind me, though. I've seen only the wrong in me, none in Giacomo. Certainly I refused to face the extent of Primo's shortcomings. I preferred to make him into what I wanted him to be, which was a loyal partner, not an adversary."

"He would never be as motivated to lead selflessly. He

doesn't carry your guilt, Sandro." She found herself moving across, wanting to impress this truth in him with a touch on his arm. "As much as it hurts you, that remorse of yours is a strength."

His face spasmed with a flash of different emotions: pain and pensive regret. A reluctant kind of acceptance. He swallowed as though he was working past deep emotion and tucked his hand against the side of her neck, thumb caressing her throat.

"I remember thinking, just after we married, that you had an original way of looking at things. I'm sorry I lost sight of that, *cara*. I won't let it happen again."

The infinitesimal threads between them, the ones that had been snapped and floating like spider silk searching for an anchor, touched and melded and began to form a bridge between them.

His expression grew even more somber and the caress on her cheek almost regretful. "You see now why I have to battle through this? Why I must refuse to step aside for Giacomo? You'll stand by me while I hold my ground?"

"I wish you'd told me all of this before." This was why he was so deeply bound to his family and why he was so closed off emotionally. To his mind, he must think giving in to his hot feelings that one time was the cause of his father's death. That's why his mother's unbridled sentimentality and grief and cries for love made him so uncomfortable. It was both a reflection of the intemperate reaction that had gripped him that day and the reason she wasn't still married to the man she had loved.

Octavia absently smoothed the wrinkle from his shirt, thinking of the weight these shoulders carried. She couldn't help but want to ease his burden. "I don't know what I can do to help," she murmured. Had he not noticed that she didn't even have the guts to defy him and strike out on her own?

"Be here," he said, the words somewhere between demand and entreaty. "Be strong with me."

She had never felt united with anyone in her life. She was needed by her son, yes, as a caregiver, but Sandro made it sound as if he wanted her to be his partner.

Her eyes dampened, she was so touched.

"If you want," she said faintly, nodding jerkily.

His breath hissed out and his mouth tilted in a relieved smile.

Such a beautiful mouth.

His smile faded and he crowded closer, leaning in—

"Oh! Excuse me! I'm so sorry," Bree blurted as she strode in. She spun to retreat just as quickly.

"Stay," Alessandro commanded, forestalling her closing the door, but keeping his arm around Octavia, allowing her to turn her blushing face into his chest. "Stay with the baby while I take Octavia down for lunch, please."

A noise of consternation escaped Octavia before she could catch it back.

"What's wrong?" he asked, tension returning in an instant. She could practically hear his *We just agreed*.

She sighed. She hadn't just been hiding from the family discord when he'd found her on the balcony.

"I have nothing to wear," she admitted.

Lunch and dinner were fairly horrible affairs and the entire day turned into one of the longest of Octavia's life. She spoke to her mother briefly, which did *not* lighten things up.

"We didn't expect you to be back this soon. I suppose we're expected to attend this birthday celebration? You'll have to make our excuses."

Apparently her grandson's birth and her daughter returning home after nearly eight months away was not inducement enough to leave the villa for a night.

Aside from Alessandro's grandfather, who was as quiet and visibly troubled as Sandro had said, everyone in the *castello* was quite unfriendly. They stopped speaking if Octavia came into a room and closed doors when she happened to pass. It was her first year at boarding school all over again.

Sandro was pulled into private conversations himself, leaving her to navigate things alone. It was exhausting and she was having serious second thoughts about all of this when she finally crawled into bed. How, exactly, did she think she was improving her circumstance by clashing with his family?

She fell into a troubled sleep and woke to feel Sandro settle behind her, carefully spooning his hot body behind hers and splaying his hand on her hip.

A racy excitement glittered through her, making her roll to face him and force a tiny space of distance before she embarrassed herself.

"What are you doing here?" she whispered.

"Coming to bed."

It was too dark to read his face, but he'd said they would sleep together once they came back to Italy. That had been the last word on the subject and it had been weeks ago. She wasn't sure she was ready.

Her body was, though. His hand went to her waist, drawing her close and in a way that was part muscle memory, her back arched and her hips wriggled so she slithered into place perfectly against his front. She shuddered with a kind of mental release as her body melted against his. It had been so long since she'd been snuggled up to his naked chest and felt his hairy legs abrade her own as he surrounded her in his strength.

She couldn't help but sigh in homecoming as she reacquainted herself with the delicious sensations of warmth and smooth skin, hard muscle and masculine scent. The dark room and soft bed gave her a safe place to forget her worries and take comfort from physical contact.

"Cara," he protested, hands moving restlessly on her, urging her to stillness. "I'm trying not to—" His breath hissed out against her cheek and he swore under his breath. "Too late."

He was hard. She could feel his erection thrusting against her abdomen, straining the silk that was trying to contain him.

"You never wear anything to bed," she murmured as she discovered his shorts.

"This way I can get up with Lorenzo. Stop," he growled, catching at her wrist. He didn't pull her hand away, however, just went very still as she traced his shape through the silk. As she rediscovered his thick length and moved the silk against the sensitive tip, he jerked against her hand. "That feels good. But you should stop." The last was a tight statement that didn't sound very sincere.

Yearning trickled through her. She longed to rediscover all the wonderful textures and scents on his body, the places that made him groan and shudder. The only time she had ever felt his equal was when she pleasured him in bed. That's why it had destroyed her to think of his seeking other women. She was supposed to be the special one, the only woman who could do this to him, make him shake and shatter.

He was a straining muscle from head to toe right now, making her believe he'd been honest with her and hadn't had any sort of release since they'd made love months ago.

"*Bella*, stop," he said in a rasp. "I'm going to come."

"I want you to," she said with a feeling in her chest like a purr. She was velvet on the inside, sensuality welling up to fill her for the first time in too long. Kissing his chest, she snaked her hand beneath his waistband, making an approving noise as she reacquainted herself with the smooth, naked shape of him, thick and taut and hard. He said something, but she only nuzzled until she found his nipple. "Do you want my mouth here?" she asked. She circled the tight bead with her tongue before sucking it wetly. "Or here?" She took firm hold of the hot, iron-hard shape of him, caressing him the way he liked, squeezing and slowly pumping.

He bit out a very dirty word, crushed her hand through the silk and thrust within her tight grip. The silk shifted against her wrist and he swelled and hardened, so fiery against her palm he burned her skin. His hand tangled in her hair and he bit out another word, her name, and lost control with a shudder, noises of satisfaction escaping him while his abdomen shuddered and lava soaked her fist.

She smiled, intensely pleased, and kept her lips pressed to where his heart slammed inside his chest while he made a gratified noise and caressed her arms and back and shoulders with shaking hands.

"I can't believe you took me apart like that," he scolded on a whisper that lilted with disbelief. He rolled away to twist his shorts down and off, using them to swipe the wetness from his belly and her hand before he tossed the garment from the bed.

Then he rolled so he hovered over her, not crushing, but close enough to be a heavy, damp, human quilt.

"I didn't know how I was going to sleep against you, but I did not expect that, you erotic little witch. I meant to behave like a gentleman." He kissed her, once briefly, then again, this time passionately and hungrily, as if they were only getting started.

Arousal spiked through her, stinging between her legs.

"Sandro, don't," she moaned, breaking away and wriggling beneath him with conflicted desire, wanting to make love, but saying, "I can't." It was just over a month and the doctor had said six weeks.

"Can't take me inside you, but I can touch you the way you just have me." In a well-practiced move, he crooked his knee to push her legs apart, then set the proprietary weight of his hand on her mound.

His hand closed into a fist, drawing the silk of her nightgown upward, bunching it to her waist. She sucked in a breath as tingles of anticipation burned, teased by the movement of his hand and the stroke of silk climbing her skin, baring her thighs.

"I didn't mean to do that to you. It just happened," she protested, shifting and trying to decide if she really wanted to fight him. He traced one fingertip along the edge of her undies, then in a delicate line down her center. She gasped and held her breath, pulsing, aching, literally throbbing for him to touch and satisfy her.

"Do you think I don't know that when you're that aggressive, you're so aroused you barely need more than a kiss? Here. Just like you did to me, *bella*," he coaxed with sultry command, sidling one fingertip beneath the narrow lace at her hip, pulling her panties askew just enough to expose her to his caress.

She held her breath as he took his time petting, parting, one fingertip gathering moisture and circling…

"Oh," she breathed.

"Let go," he whispered, covering her mouth with a tender kiss as he explored more intently.

She sobbed with pleasure, not realizing how aroused

she was until she found release under the lightest of caresses, losing control in an abrupt shiver of pure ecstasy.
Oh, she had missed this. So much, so much.

Their kiss continued with both of them making satis-
fied noises in their throats as he continued to caress her,
soothing and bringing her down from the heights.

"Now sleep, before I eat you alive," he insisted, replac-
ing her undies and drawing her body tight against his. He
was aroused again—still?—but only tucked her head under
his chin. "You're delicious, my adorable wife. I'd make
love to you the rest of the night, if I could."

She wanted to keep making love. By the end of their
honeymoon, they'd been insatiable, sometimes spending
all day in bed pleasuring each other to exhaustion.

Had she really believed she could leave him and never
know this again?

For the first time in months, her heart felt full and her
ache of scorn dissipated. Her lashes dampened with relief
at being held this closely against him while the tingles of
climax left her floating. She fell asleep feeling treasured
and safe.

Then rose to feed Lorenzo early in the morning, coming
back to their room to find Alessandro showered, shaved
and dressed in a suit and tie.

Leaving.

CHAPTER EIGHT

"YOU'RE LEAVING?" SHE SNAPPED out of her sleepy state, forgetting about crawling back into their warm bed and rekindling that close feeling from last night, so angry, so *betrayed*, she could only stand there hugging her arms across this stupid, flimsy nightgown she'd let him lift last night.

"If you hold off reacting until—"

"Don't tell me not to react! Failing to tell you how I felt left me stuck in London with the wrong baby! No, Sandro. Not fair," she railed. "You're treating me like a woman you picked up for the night, tearing out of here without even a promise to call."

"I'm going downstairs," he said through his teeth. "For breakfast. You don't trust me at all, do you?" He was affronted, glaring as though he really expected better of her.

So maybe she was going zero to sixty and should slow down. "You're not going into the city?"

His gaze shuttered and he tugged the cuff of his suit coat. "Not until later."

She moved to pick up the silky wrap that matched her nightgown, pulling it on in a swirl and tying it off. "I'm not a bitch to be left in the kennel, you know." Oh, it felt good to say what she thought. "What was that?" She pointed with accusation at the twisted sheets. "Was it just something to sweeten me up so I wouldn't be upset this morning?"

"You started that," he shot back. "And I am more than happy to stage a do-over if it *will* sweeten you up."

She glared daggers into him, letting him see every last ounce of her fury.

The tails of his suit jacket bunched over his wrists as he pushed his hands in his pockets, but he wasn't as unperturbed as he was trying to pretend. His hands had formed fists in those pockets and his jaw was like iron. He was just as mad and refusing to show it.

"I wasn't going to leave this room until I'd spoken to you," he said, tone pithy, then firm. "I'd like you to come down, too, as soon as you can be ready."

"Why?" She glanced at the clock. "It's not even seven."

"I know, but Nonno is making an announcement once everyone else comes down. I want us there when he does. We're not going back to the town house, *cara*. We're living here from now on."

"What?" Of all the things he might have said… "Are you serious?" She moved to the bed and sank onto the edge, drawing the blankets over her legs, feeling cold. Stunned. "Really? What about…?" She couldn't even compute how many people this would affect. "This is not going to halt a mutiny," she told him.

"I was shocked when he suggested it last night, too. I only asked him whether he thought he'd set up false expectations, letting Giacomo move in when he was campaigning for election. He hadn't expected them to stay on, he said, or that my cousins would inveigle their way into moving in, but…they're family. He sees now that his generosity has created a gray area."

She supposed it was better for Ermanno to announce his wishes now than for Alessandro to inherit sometime in the future and then what? Turn everyone out at that point? That really would be a mess.

"Where will they go?"

"They have homes. Some are rented out." He shrugged, not saying aloud that they were collecting income while living off Ermanno's good graces. "I'll be offering the town house to Giacomo until they are able to move back into their own. That's one of the reasons I'm going into the city, to set up the movers, along with finalizing the restructuring at the office. I'm not leaving you in a kennel, Octavia," he added with disdain. "Kindly don't insult me like that again. I'm asking you to stay here as a statement that this is our home now. This is where I live with my wife and son."

She could only stare at him, hands squeezing her knees while she took in that running his town house was nothing compared to overseeing the running of a house this size on a huge estate with a working winery among other things. The task intimidated her down to the bottoms of her bare feet.

"Will your grandfather stay here with us? To run the estate?" *Please say yes.*

"I've asked him to, but he wants to move into his grandmother's rooms attached to the old stable house. We'll have to take a hard look at its condition. My sisters used it as a playroom when we were young. It may be three or four months before he actually makes the move, but he seemed determined."

"I don't know what to say." She really didn't.

"You could say that you understand and agree." He ambled the few steps to bring himself to stand in front of her, then he caught her wrist and drew her to stand. He hooked his arm around her and pulled her tight against his tailored clothes. "You could say that you'll come downstairs and stand beside me. If you wanted to add that last night was as good for you as it was for me, I'd like to hear that, too."

She blushed, but he kissed her, not letting her talk as he made her remember exactly why she hadn't been able to keep her hands off him. With a moan, she softened under his hard kiss, smoothing her hands up the stiff fabric of his jacket to curl around his neck.

He smelled good and molded her against him with that confident way of his, making the silk she wore grow warm and slide against her skin, turning her on even more.

But he wasn't trying to manage her. With his own swift loss of control last night, he'd made it clear he was as reactive to her as she was to him. He wasn't trying to persuade a pawn right now. They were equals in bed, and he was asking her to be his partner out of it.

Her heart swelled and she encouraged him to play out their long, passionate kiss, rubbing against him invitingly as she felt his arousal.

He pressed her away with a warning flashing in his gaze. "I'll need another cold shower at this rate. Will you dress and come down?"

"They're going to hate me," she sighed, but lowered to flat feet and moved into the walk-in closet. Of course she would accompany him. It wasn't just for Lorenzo, either. It was for Sandro. For this marriage they were trying to save.

She wanted to save it, she admitted tentatively to herself.

"I sent an email to Michaela to come and fit you with a new wardrobe," he said, following to lean in the doorway as she started to remove the overwrap for her nightdress. "You'll need something for Nonno's birthday anyway."

"Thank you." She paused with the open ties in her hands, glancing at him.

He made no move to leave, looking very comfortable leaning there.

"Is that all?" she asked.

"Unless you have something."

"No, I'll be ready in fifteen minutes or so."

"Good." Still he didn't move.

She folded her arms. "Are you planning to stand there and watch me change?"

"Yes."

"No," she assured him, moving forward to press him out of the closet. "You're not."

"We have been married too long for shyness," he argued, refusing to be budged, hands finding her hips and straying freely.

She caught them and pushed them off her. "Go have a baby and come back and talk to me about shyness." She applied her full weight to his shoulder, pushing until he made a *tsk* noise and backed out of the doorway.

"You're being silly. You're beautiful," he told her.

She pulled the door closed to lock him out.

His blurry silhouette remained on the far side of the frosted glass. She stayed where she was, watching him.

He stepped closer, one hand pressing so his fingertips were a half circle of dots, as if he was trying to touch her through the barrier. "Octavia." That was his sex voice and sent the best kind of shivers down her spine. "I wish we'd had the lights on last night. I liked everything I felt."

A giddy happiness broke open inside her, making her smile wobble as she admitted breathlessly, "I did, too."

He stood there a moment, as if he might be willing her to come out again. She was tempted, but then he finally said, "You'll meet me downstairs?"

"Fifteen minutes," she promised.

"Grazie." He left.

While she stood at the door much as he had, as though she was waiting for this translucent barrier to dissipate so she could be with him and finally see him clearly.

Alessandro meant to spend the week in town, but he felt a lingering unease where his wife was concerned. Despite the delicious physical connection they'd enjoyed the other night, her leap to suspicions in the morning told him she still didn't trust him. As he spoke to her through the week, she reminded him of the woman she was in London, offering facts with very little editorial.

It made him dwell on the conversation with his grandfather that had kept him up late their first night here.

"Your father taught me to let my son make his own choices, so I will support all the decisions you've made, Sandro," Ermanno had said.

"You were furious at some of the choices Papa made," Sandro had scoffed. "Eloping with my mother…"

His grandfather had swept his hand through the air. "Her family was…well, you know we've had to carry some of them at different times. And her capricious ways…" He shook his head. "Such a wild little bird." But there was fondness in his papery voice.

"She's bringing her new fiancé to your party. She wants your blessing. I couldn't talk her out of it," Sandro warned. "If you want me to—"

"No, no. I would like to see her," Ermanno insisted. "She'll have my blessing. She loved my son." His grandfather's eyes had gone watery and sincere. "And she gave you to me, even left you here when she went off to marry her Englishman. I have come to love her like my own daughter. I was angry with your father for marrying her, but now I'm grateful. And I worry for you, because Octavia doesn't love you."

Sandro's heart had derailed in his chest.

"Yet," his grandfather had added, voice distant and muffled in the rush that filled Sandro's ears. "Your wife can come to love you, Sandro. Mine did." His grandfather sobered with the grief he still felt nearly ten years after Nonna had passed away. "If you let her."

The anguish in his grandfather's face hadn't been an advertisement for the joys of love. More like a cautionary tale.

Sandro didn't want the sort of vulnerability that came with loving, but he had never disregarded his grandfather's wisdom in his life. It wasn't as though Octavia had asked him for love, though. She'd made a point of telling him it wasn't required. If she wasn't prepared to risk her heart, that was good, because neither was he.

He wanted her trust, though, and told himself it would come with time. Today he had news that he hoped would put the worst of their conflict behind them.

"You came home for a swim?" she asked as he found her new swimsuit and dug out his own. "It's a nice day, but not that nice. Have they even readied the pool yet?"

He shook his head. "Not here. Is he done?" He grinned at the drunken look on his son's face as he finished nursing. Sandro tossed the suits on the bed, then scooped up Lorenzo to burp him. "*Scusi, figlio*, you'll have to stay home," he said, patting the baby's back. "Too hot for you. I looked it up."

"What is?" Octavia asked, holding up her swimsuit and wrinkling her nose at the thought of wearing it.

Sandro wanted it to be a surprise. Thirty minutes later, they were in a private water taxi, puttering through the towering cliffs of a narrow gorge to the baths carved by ancient Romans into the rock walls. By then she had figured out where they were going and the hot springs were a lovely treat, but—

"You should have told me before we left the house. I wouldn't have worn my new ring," Octavia said as she came out of her changing room, a towel wrapped over her modest two-piece.

The humid air was warm and the blue water inside the cave misty and inviting. Only a handful of people were here, all tucked in private corners, but she hadn't wanted to leave the ring in her changing room.

She tilted the blue sapphire that had arrived hours after Alessandro had gone into the city the other morning. It sat where her wedding rings still didn't quite fit.

"I'll be terrified the whole time that it will slip off and I'll lose it," she said.

"I noticed it before we left, but I didn't want you to take it off. I don't like seeing you without my ring." He brought the knuckle of her finger to his lips. "I'm possessive."

Octavia made a noise. She knew that much about him, she thought wryly, but curled her fingers inside his loose grasp, thinking about what had happened when the ring had arrived at the house.

Her troubled thoughts must have shown in her face because Sandro asked stiffly, "You don't like it?"

"What? No, I love it. I told you I did when it arrived," she reminded, pulling her hand from his to ensure the stone was perfectly centered. "It was just that when Viviana saw it…" She couldn't hide her distaste at how Primo's family was treating her. "She asked if it was a push present."

"A push—?"

"A gift from a husband to his wife for pushing out a baby. She said I didn't deserve one because the surgeons did all the work."

She stepped into the pool and silky heat washed over her calves, soothing her prickly mood.

Alessandro halted beside her. "Your coolness the last few days begins to make sense. She'll apologize," he said tightly.

"Is that why you brought me here? You thought I needed warming up?" she asked. Twisting her mouth to the side, she scrunched her nose at him. "I wasn't trying to avoid you, but I didn't want to tell you. I was pretty rude. But I had had it with the way they're all acting toward me, Sandro! She sounded just like Primo. I knew that was the source of it and I just snapped."

His brows went up. "What did you do?"

"Stooped to her level." She swept her towel off and tossed it to the edge, then sank quickly into the blissfully hot water, turning so she still faced him, but was hidden to her shoulders. "I told her that she might want to consider who I sleep with, since she's asked you to underwrite that tanning salon of hers."

Sandro slowly came down the steps after her, not sinking into the water, not taking his gaze off hers. He was wearing his disapproving look, but she didn't know if it was for her or his cousin.

"She told me not to expect you to fight my battles and I said fine. She was right. That I have no right to interfere in your business decisions, but that she can't expect to enjoy the hospitality of someone she is insulting. I said that if she needed help packing, she should let me know since I'd be more than happy to arrange assistance from *my* staff."

She ended with a press of her lips and a sheepish look up at him.

He folded his arms, looking so much sexier than she felt. His chest was gorgeous, his shoulders a sculptor's curved line that begged to be traced with fingertips and lips. He dropped his hands to his hips, framing his perfect torso with his neatly muscled arms.

"No, I didn't bring you here to warm you up, but I did wonder if something was bothering you. I also wanted to take us out of the house for a few hours. Primo has been in touch with Nonno. He's trying to go over my head and my grandfather has told him he can't. Nonno is drawing up a settlement that will help Primo pay his legal bills, but he will forfeit any claim to the estate. Primo has accepted and that puts an end to any aspirations his side of the clan has. I expect they'll be gone by the time we get home today. It's the final nail in the coffin, if you will."

He scowled into the middle distance and she could almost hear his thoughts. He'd caused the death of his own father and hadn't been disinherited, but Primo was losing virtually everything over what he'd done.

But Sandro's mistake had been a youthful accident, Primo's a deliberate act with intent to harm.

She stood without thinking and moved to wrap her arms around her husband's waist. He closed his arms across her back, hand smoothing over her bare skin, fingers going under the wide band of her shoulder strap.

A second later, she felt a stirring of his flesh just below the line of the water. He set her back a step, expression wry. "Swimming was a bad idea. I was only thinking about the view…" He roamed his gaze down her bare upper chest and arms. The wet swimsuit plastered against her breasts revealed a *lot* more than it hid. "I didn't consider the effect it would have on me."

She fell back, sending her hands forward to splash water into his face.

The rest of the week was less stressful and by the end of it, Alessandro hung back in the city just long enough for a fresh haircut and a barber's shave before he put on his tuxedo and left the town house for good. And without regret. As difficult as these recent weeks had been, as much as he was still ironing out wrinkles across the organization, he had never felt as sure in his role. Any lingering misgivings he'd had about controlling the Ferrante fortune were gone.

He was its caretaker for the future and held the entire organization in a firm, unapologetic grasp.

Now he was entering the home that was his. His grandfather would live with them until late spring. Octavia had encouraged Ermanno to stay in the main house as long as possible, to help her learn the running of things. Ermanno was in his element as a mentor so Alessandro expected great things to come from their budding relationship.

Tonight marked the launch of their new life together.

He entered their suite in high spirits and two things happened. First, he was knocked breathless by the sight of her.

He'd told her stylist, Michaela, to bring jewel tones. He always preferred stronger colors on his wife than the pastels she gravitated toward. The gown she'd chosen was black velvet with a skirt of sapphire blue. The top clung lovingly to her ample breasts and tied behind her neck, leaving her back and shoulders covered only by the loose curls of her long, dark hair. The fall of blue draped in flattering lines over her round hips. Tall heels gave her the ultrafeminine sexiness that every man enjoyed. He wanted to tumble her to the bed and forget the guests arriving downstairs.

But it wasn't just her beauty that struck him. It was her. He was glad to see her. He'd missed her. He waited for her to come across like in the old days and slide her arms around him. They had come that far, hadn't they?

"I just fed Lorenzo. Almost ready," she said with barely

a glance at him, head bent and attention on her phone as she tapped out a message.

Apparently, they hadn't.

He frowned, wondering who she could possibly be texting so feverishly. She made a final strike and it whooshed, but at the same time released a ringtone chime.

Octavia read it and let out a delighted laugh.

Alessandro was taken aback. That rich sound was something he hadn't heard in... He didn't know how long. Far too long. It was like birdsong in spring, promising and filling him with hope.

Her smile, so genuine, took her look of aloof sophistication to a level of sparkling beauty that did more than knock him breathless. It kicked him in the heart. He hadn't seen her happy like this since before she had gone to London.

And someone else had made it happen.

The jealousy that blindsided him in that moment was as shocking as it was severe. He didn't mean to sound so harsh when he said, "Who is that?" but he must have because she sobered quickly, face going into that neutral mask that tucked all her thoughts and feelings away.

"Sorcha," she replied, spine stiffening defensively. "Why?"

"Sorcha? The woman from the hospital?" He subtly recoiled. His shame over how his cousin's subterfuge had affected the stranger was only eclipsed by his remorse over the damage done to his wife and marriage.

"We've stayed in touch," Octavia said with a cool click of the button to blacken her screen, setting the phone face-down on a side table.

"Why?" He couldn't see any sense in it.

"Because she's a new mother like me. I can ask her about rash creams and growth spurts, things no one else wants to talk about."

"Bree knows about those things. Ask her."

"She doesn't have a baby. It's different. And I like hearing how Enrique is doing," Octavia stated, setting her chin stubbornly. "Why do you disapprove?"

He heard the frost in her tone and realized he had to tread carefully. "I didn't say I don't approve, only that I don't understand," he prevaricated.

"Exactly. She does. We're in the same boat. I was telling her that I had this party to go to, but that I was tired because it was another rough night with Lorenzo. She's supposed to be organizing a gala, but isn't up to starting because she's tired, too."

"And you were laughing about that?"

"Not exactly. I asked her if it was too late for her to take Lorenzo so I could get a good night's sleep. She texted at the same time, wondering if I still wanted Enrique because he's been so colicky. Perhaps it's bad taste to make jokes about what happened, but…" She sighed and flipped her hair. "It's nice to have a friend with a baby the same age. I'm not going to stop talking to her. She needs me as much as I need her."

Beneath her defiance was a disturbing hint of loneliness. It twisted Sandro's insides.

"I wouldn't ask you to," he assured her, moving across in a deliberate effort to close the distance. "I'm not ready to laugh about the baby swap," he admitted darkly. "But I take your joking as a sign that you're putting it in the past and I'm glad." He rubbed her arms, admitting, "I was of the mind that we'd never have to face her again, which suited me. Those days at the hospital were not my finest hour. If I sounded disapproving, that's where it was coming from."

She regarded him solemnly before she said, "I can appreciate that, but I wouldn't feel right cutting ties. I…had a friend at boarding school. We didn't really have much in common except we were both going through a spell of defying our parents."

He lifted his brows, curious about that, but she cut her gaze away and shrugged off providing details.

"She wound up expelled and her parents disowned her. I tried to help, brought her home for the holidays, but my parents strongly encouraged me to end that friendship if I wanted to continue enjoying the limited freedoms I had." Her smile was bitter. "I still gave her money when she asked, but I know she wound up taking lovers just to have a bed at night. I've never felt right about not making more of an effort to help her."

She lifted her thick lashes so her gaze came up while her chin stayed down, framing her abashed mink brown eyes.

He wanted to ask more about her own acts of defiance, but stayed on topic. "Sorcha needs your help?" he surmised.

She shrugged one bare shoulder. "I'm not sure. She hasn't said much except that Cesar didn't know about Enrique. It's been quite hard for her, I think. Don't be judgy," she added swiftly.

"Of course not," he murmured, dismissing the other woman from his mind as the one before him, the one that mattered, was confiding in a way that was deeply encouraging. He closed his hands on her waist and drew her against him. "I'm sorry you haven't been sleeping. I'm here now to get up with him and you know Bree's always happy to help. We'll make your excuses as early as we can tonight, even though I'll be sorry to let you go. You look beautiful." He leaned to kiss her.

"Lipstick," she said, averting her mouth from his. "Putting on my makeup took twice as long as it should have. Don't make me start again."

He picked up her hands, smiling through his disappointment while an odd sensation moved through him. Admiration and warmth at what a loyal person she was, but something deeper and brighter. He kissed her fingers, habitually trying to resist whatever that rush of emotion was simply because it was stronger than he liked to allow.

"Come," he said with a tug of her hand toward the door. "I want to dance with my wife."

Friends and neighbors and local dignitaries were here to help Ermanno celebrate, but it was more of a family reunion. The bulk of the guests were Ferrantes. Aunts and uncles and cousins galore. All of Sandro's sisters were here and even his mother had arrived in a gushing stir of effervescent excitement, making the crowd part and look. Ysabelle greeted Octavia like she hadn't seen her in ages, then moved on to hug her daughters and would likely embrace every single person in the room before the night was over.

Octavia smiled. Sandro muttered something about needing a drink and excused himself, leaving Octavia with his eldest sister, Antonia, and her husband. Antonia was only a year younger than Sandro and had married at eighteen. Their fourth child was currently swelling the front of her gown.

"I'm curious," Octavia admitted, taking advantage of this moment without Sandro's listening ears. "Did you all get your father's temperament? Your mother is so demonstrative, but you all seem so reserved by comparison."

Antonia's husband made a choking noise and gave his wife a look. "I'll help Sandro with the drinks," he said circumspectly and disappeared.

Antonia chuckled. "We tone ourselves down around Sandro. He hates it when we yell or cry or get excited. Actually, Papa was just as exuberant. He and Mamma had huge, passionate fights all the time."

"And that scarred Sandro?" Octavia asked.

"Oh, no," Antonia dismissed. "It didn't bother any of us. We knew they loved each other. They would tell us, 'I love him but he's being stubborn' or 'I love her but she's being unreasonable.' And then doors would slam and they would yell some more and finally kiss and make up. No, it was the way Papa died that changed Sandro." Her eyes glossed with old grief. "We were all heartbroken and Sandro felt terribly guilty. To be honest, he had the worst temper of all of us before that. Kept the highest standards, argued the most determinedly for whatever he thought was right. He feels things very, very deeply. That's why Papa's death nearly destroyed him. He still blames himself. He always will."

Antonia's lips trembled.

"I shouldn't have brought it up." Octavia's heart ached for Sandro. She thought of all those times he'd said to a wound-up Primo, *"Relax. Come into my office and let's talk about it."* She'd always felt shut out of their important discussions, but he'd really been calming his cousin from doing something rash.

Understanding didn't reduce her concern, however. It just made her realize how thoroughly he'd locked away his deepest feelings.

"It's fine," Antonia murmured. "I just try not to show how sad I still am if Sandro is around. He takes it so hard. And it's not that he became controlling after Papa died, but he became very controlled and expected us to be the same. If he overheard an argument, he moved in to defuse it. He would lecture us to think first. Bad things can happen if you don't, you know? Mamma dealt with her grief the other way, by letting every thought and feeling out. She married the viscount, trying to find what she'd had with Papa and even though the viscount loved her right up until the day he died, he never really knew how to deal with her. Not many men know how to match that much heartfelt expression."

Octavia watched Ysabelle snuggling up to her Spanish count as she introduced him to Ermanno. "It must have felt like two extremes," she mused.

"It was, and it was comforting to have Sandro's steady counterbalance while she was going through all those highs and lows." Antonia cast an affectionate look across the room to where Sandro was speaking to an elderly couple. "He made sure we all learned to control ourselves, and we still do around him. He has no idea how passionately we fight with our husbands," she confided cheekily, nodding toward her own. "That's why mine nearly swallowed his tongue when you said I was reserved. I have a terrible temper. But it feels so good to let it out." She patted her round belly and grinned. "And the makeup sex is always fun, too."

Octavia blushed, glimpsing Ysabelle in her daughter as Antonia overshared, but it was nice, too. It made her feel closer to her sister-in-law.

She was still thinking about makeup sex when she slid back into bed next to Sandro after feeding Lorenzo at dawn. Sandro was fast asleep, having come to bed only a few hours ago, waiting until the last guest had gone. He was on his stomach, sheet at his waist, sculpted shoulders and back bare to the stripes of rosy light coming through the blinds.

She longed to touch him, longed to make up with him properly. She wanted to kiss better all the hurts and misunderstandings and lack of communication. Maybe lovemaking wasn't love, but it was connection and caring and the opposite of fighting. She wanted harmony.

A real, true, fresh beginning.

Lifting her hand, she hesitated, briefly unsure, but didn't let herself overthink it. The line of his spine begged to be traced and she did, nudging the sheet a little lower on the curve of his buttocks, then coming back up to the edge of his fresh haircut and the shadow that had come in on his jaw.

He drew in a long breath, big body stirring as he opened one eye. "Is he crying?"

"No," she said softly, feeling defenseless as she said, "He's fast asleep."

And because he was a very smart man, he didn't ask her why she'd woken him. He read the want that she didn't try to disguise and lifted his arm to gather her and pull her half under him. "Is he?"

She felt him thicken against her thigh as he pressed over her. He hadn't even kissed her, but he was instantly aroused. His body was smooth and hard and strapping, his neck still faintly scented with his cologne, his chest hot and hard against her kiss.

Liquid heat rolled through her veins as they shifted to lie stomach to stomach, chin to chin. The contact made her sleepy muscles feel even more like melted wax. As they kissed lazily and moved against each other, her nightgown climbed. He slid his hand up her thigh and stroked her hip, her waist, her lower back and bottom, her spine and rib cage and then, ah, yes. Her breast.

He was gentle and possessive and it felt so good she had to moan and bring her knee up to his hip and press with her calf against the back of his thigh, encouraging him to position himself to rub against her.

"I have always thought you had beautiful breasts, but, *cara*..." He dragged her nightgown up and off. "Oh, *bella*." He kissed the swell and admired how it overflowed his hand, thumb circling her nipple so it was a firm, eager point.

The sweetest nerve endings tightened in her inner thighs as he played, making her ache for his touch. His thrust.

He was wearing his silk boxers again, but she could feel the insistence of him against her as if one move was all that was needed and he'd rip through silk and be inside her. She could hardly breathe she was so gripped by anticipation, but…

"I should tell you," she murmured, self-conscious, but unable to keep from caressing his chest, tracing the pattern of hair and splaying her hand down his waist. "The books said it might hurt at first, so, um, can you be careful?"

He drew back. "I thought we were just fooling around. It hasn't been six weeks."

"It's close enough," she grumbled. "That was just a recommendation. The doctor said if I felt like it sooner, I could, but to use condoms. There are some in the drawer."

His brows went up and he rolled away to look, almost as if he didn't believe her. When he came back with the little square in his hand, his eyes were pure green and brilliant with desire. "If I'm dreaming, I'd better not wake up."

She smiled until he kissed her again, then she couldn't do anything but respond to the deep, drugging way he made love to her mouth. They kissed for a long time, as if this was all they were planning to do. He wove his fingers into her hair and she traced light fingertips over his throat and shoulders and up to where their lips devoured each other.

She loved that he wasn't rushing her. In fact, it was as though he was returning to a place he'd almost forgotten and had to make a point of touching each inch of her skin, inhaling deeply near her ear, licking at her neck and backing off to watch as he stroked his hands over her. He was focused wholly on her, bringing her hand to his heart, kissing her temple and collarbone, then the inside of her elbow. He glanced to see if she liked his lips on the underside of her breast, against her scar, on her inner thighs and against the lace of her panties.

She swallowed, moved and aroused, trembling as she met his gaze, so steady and yet so emotive. She'd thought him adept. A playboy. A practiced seducer. He was, but this wasn't a routine. He wanted to pleasure her. She saw earnestness in him. A desire for forgiveness.

This was more than a physical reacquainting. It was reconciliation.

She touched his face, memorizing his features with her eyes and her touch. He pursed his lips against her thumb pad, seeming in agreement that they had time, lots of time. That reassured her in a way nothing else could.

When he started to peel her panties away, she lifted her hips, modesty tossed away with the blue silk. Unashamed as he admired her.

Kneeling between her legs he pushed off his boxers, sending them to the floor before he covered himself and lowered to settle over her. She lifted again, seeking and inviting his penetration where she was wet and so needy.

He groaned as he kissed her and started to press into her.

"Oh!" she said, startled by the sting.

The noise he made was pure, maddened pain. He rolled away and threw his arm over his eyes.

"Sandro—"

"Give me a minute, *cara*," he said, voice tight.

"I was only going to say it's not that bad. I want to. I want *you*." She splayed her torso over his, sliding against him in a full-body caress. "Please."

He made another agonized noise and said, "I'm the one

who wants to beg, *cara*. Like this then." He dragged her to straddle him. "You do it. Go as slowly as you need." He spoke through his teeth, not even opening his eyes, and reached up to catch his hands under the edge of the ornate headboard.

She took a moment to admire the taut strip of muscle he made, straining beneath her, nipples hard and jaw clenched. Then she guided him and took a few careful inhales and exhales as she brought him into her. When she was seated right against him, his thick shape filling her like the pulse of her own heart, she gloried in the perfection of it.

She stroked her hands over his hard chest and his rib cage swelled under her touch, breath moving through his teeth in hisses of tested control.

It made her smile. So much man. So much discipline held so very, very tightly.

So unwilling to let himself let go.

Bracing her hands on his chest, she scraped her nails into his hard pecs, liking the way he shivered like a stallion feeling spurs. Could she crack his restraint?

"You've always been the one to call the shots," she mused, moving experimentally. So much pleasure sparked through her, she gasped and almost lost the plot.

His eyes opened in glittering slits of green. "You're enjoying this," he gritted out.

Her smile widened. "That's the point, isn't it?" She moved with more purpose, teasing them both, arching as another streak that was even more intense went through her.

His nostrils flared and he brought his hands to her hips, fingers flexing in with warning, abdomen sucked tight as he cautioned her to take care with her movements. "*Dio*, you're beautiful, riding me like this."

"So are you," she allowed, moving in a way that was absolute joy, hips undulating instinctively. Irrepressibly. "I missed this, *caro*," she confessed in an unrestrained whisper, growing greedy. "So much. And I want you to—" Her voice caught as climax rose hot and fast. "Oh, Sandro," she breathed.

"Yes," he growled. "Let it happen." He lifted beneath her, maintaining the surging rhythm, driving her over the edge. She arched her back, not caring that he watched as her breasts flushed and trembled and she shuddered atop him, sobs of ecstasy escaping her parted lips.

Her cries died away and her bones dissolved.

"Come here," he commanded. His hand slid up to curl around her neck and bring her down, then tangled in her hair as they kissed deeply, bodies moving in gentle adjustment. "Your hair," he muttered, burying his nose in a handful of it as it fell across his face.

"I'm sorry—"

"No, I adore it. I want to feel it all over me. I want you like this, naked and hot around me, all the damned time. I missed this, too," he said fiercely.

"You were supposed to come with me," she pouted. Damn his control. She tested the sandpapery roughness of his cheek with her fingertips, unable to be truly disappointed when she felt this good and he was still hard inside her, promising another release just like the first.

With a little purr of adulation, she blanketed herself over him and took possession of his throat with openmouthed kisses.

"Make love to me again. Take me with you this time." His hand shook as he smoothed her hair back from the side of her face so he could look into her eyes.

She felt sultry and seductive and powerful as she sat up. She was used to the stretch inside her now and began

to move without restraint, wantonly, determined to un-
ravel his willpower one rock of her hips at a time. Her
skin dampened, his teeth bared, the pleasure climbed and
she felt as though she was drowning in the tropical sea
of his eyes.

"Now," she told him as the waves of expansion washed
up from where they were locked together. Her mouth
opened in a silent scream and he pressed her hard onto
his hips, thrusting up to her, releasing ragged cries of ab-
ject pleasure.

This time when she sank down to let her breasts flatten against his chest, he twisted her beneath him, withdrawing carefully before aligning her half under him, his
breath still coming in pants against her cheek.

She nuzzled the prickling stubble on his chin and bit at
his lips with her own.

"*Mia bella moglie*," he breathed, snuggling her naked
body to his own. "That was perfect. Utterly perfect."

Not quite. He was still too contained, but they were
closer than they'd been.

CHAPTER NINE

SANDRO COULDN'T RECALL having spent any real time with Octavia's parents. His dealings with her father, Mario Benevento, had left him with an impression of a shrewd businessman. They'd hammered out the marriage contracts as objectively as any other business deal would be negotiated.

As for her mother, Trista, he recalled her coming to dinner with Mario at the *castello* only the once. Sandro's mother and grandfather had been there with Giacomo and his wife. Primo had been there, too, along with a handful of others. If Trista had said more than a few words, he couldn't recall what they were.

He'd spoken to his in-laws at the wedding, of course, even danced with his mother-in-law. Once he and Octavia settled into the town house, he recalled mentioning that they should have her parents to dinner. Octavia had said something about asking when they might be available.

They must not have been, Sandro now realized, because he had never sat at a table with just the two of them. He would have remembered an evening this painful.

It didn't help that his respect for Mario had fallen into the gutter weeks ago, after Octavia had opened up and called the man a cheat, then plummeted further when she confided they'd forced her to end a friendship. Sandro had already thought Mario a chauvinist, but he now saw the man was an outright sexist without any sensitivity genes at all. He monopolized the conversation with politics and business, not asking his daughter how she was recovering from Lorenzo's birth and not giving his wife opportunities to address personal topics, either. He loved his wine and had taken little notice of his grandson.

Thankfully dinner was almost over. Dessert had arrived. The baked half pear was stuffed with walnuts and honey. A ball of gelato next to it held a sprig of mint. All the food had been excellent. Sandro might have enjoyed himself if it had just been a date with his wife, but he had to tolerate *this*.

"Did you bring a copy of the DNA report? I want one for my files before we officiate the hand off," Mario said as the summary of his latest and greatest executive decisions came to an end.

Across from him, Octavia paused with her spoon halfway to her mouth.

"I had some notarized copies made," Sandro said smoothly. "But we can discuss all of that at the office sometime next week. I'll have my PA call yours to set it up."

"That's not why you're here tonight?" Mario said with a degree of incredulity.

"No, this is a social call," Sandro said. He looked across at Octavia, unsure why that wouldn't be clear. "Octavia wanted to visit and introduce you to your grandson."

Which wasn't quite true. He had suggested it and she had made the arrangements with a mutter about inevitability and her mother not being happy. Now her dark gaze met his, black-coffee eyes turbulent in her otherwise expressionless face. In the past few days, she'd been quick to smile and reach out to him, but tonight she was the pretty mannequin again.

Mario snorted. "There was no need to rush that. Boy won't speak for years."

Octavia's fingers tightened around her spoon.

Sandro was offended on their son's behalf, too. And Octavia's. This was a stark glimpse at the sort of disconnected childhood she had hinted at. He had to catch himself from turning on Mario with a few home truths.

As it turned out, he didn't have to react. Octavia blurted, "Even longer before he's allowed to."

A moment of stunned silence, then Mario said, "What did you say?" in a tone infused with ominous warning.

"Octavia," her mother scolded in a murmur.

"No, I'm going to say it," Octavia said on a burst of suppressed wrath. "He put you through all those miscarriages, insisted he wanted a boy, I finally deliver one and he can't even be bothered to hold him. I don't understand you." Her voice rose as she leveled the last at her father.

"Cara," Sandro said gently, trying to keep this from becoming a scene.

"An heir and a *spare*, Octavia. That's what I need." Mario turned his red face to Sandro. "And so do you if you want to finalize the merger. Control your wife."

Sandro took issue. Very strong issue, but Octavia went off enough for both of them.

"Really?" she cried, rising to toss her napkin over her dessert. "All this time and you still don't understand how biology works? What if I don't have another boy? What if I don't want to go through another pregnancy? What happens to the merger then?"

"The inheritance moves through regular channels," Sandro interjected, taking satisfaction from throwing the reminder in his father-in-law's face. "It will go to your mother, you, then any children we have. Stopping with Lorenzo would only delay my takeover, not prevent it. And we should get him home to bed," he added, rising to move to the door of the dining room where he requested their car be brought around and that Bree put the baby into it.

"Yes. Leave. Come back when you've found your manners," Mario said patronizingly.

"Why on earth would I ever come back?" Octavia cried. "I married the man you chose for me— No! I married a man *better* than the one you chose for me, and you've never so much as said, 'Thank you.' Now I deliver an heir and you turn your nose up. Do you think I want my son near a man incapable of showing either of us a shred of affection or respect? No. I don't. Mamma may come and see Lorenzo anytime she likes, but you will never see me or my son again. You have nothing I want, especially your precious money. Give it to Sandro, spend it, throw it in the bay. Do whatever will make you happy with it because it's obviously the only thing that ever will."

"Buonanotte," Sandro said, gathering his wife and shuffling her out of the room.

"Don't act like I'm the one behaving badly. He deserves to hear this. Or are you worried I'm ruining your secret backdoor deals?" She pulled away from him as they reached the front door.

"There is nothing secret about any of it," he stated, not liking her accusation. "You never asked." He dropped her coat on her shoulders and pressed her outside.

She shoved her hands into the sleeves and folded the edges over herself before throwing herself into the back of the car.

He went around the other side and climbed in, regretting they didn't have a privacy window. "We talked about having three or four children before we married," he reminded.

"Pregnancies," she snapped.

"*Si*. You're right. I take the hopeful view that all of your pregnancies will be successful. Sue me for being an optimist. And the gender doesn't matter. Your father wanted to make it a condition they be boys, but I struck that. I begin the takeover with the birth of our first child and assume majority control with our second. We needed a trigger of some kind for these things. In the unlikely event we had no children, he very rightly made provisions to maintain control and leave his fortune to his family through his estate."

"It's all just business," she jeered.

"Yes," he bit out. "It was."

Octavia fumed at him across the peaceful baby sleeping between them. Their *trigger*.

Her mother, at least, had held Lorenzo. Her expression had even softened a bit. While Octavia had stood there waiting for her father to say something like, *Good job. Thank you. I'm so proud of you. So pleased for you.*

But there'd been nothing.

She'd spent the next hour realizing what a tremendous fool she'd been for ever imagining she could earn something from him beyond a flickering glance of disappointment. When he had dismissed her son as something he didn't want to see *for years*, she had reached her limit.

The fact that Sandro had hustled her out of there before she really told her father what she thought of him was infuriating. She had nearly a quarter century of resentment stockpiled and was eager to let it out.

"I have a right to be angry," she told him when she entered their suite after tucking Lorenzo into the proper nursery they'd had fashioned for him across the hall.

"Because I signed contracts a year ago that you don't like?" He set aside his phone with a rattle onto the night table and shrugged out of his jacket, tossing it over the back of the nearest chair.

"Because you won't let me be angry!" She kicked off her shoes in the middle of the floor and began pulling out her earrings, dropping them into the dish on the vanity table. "I don't care about the stupid contracts and how you and my father planned to transfer control of his all-important fortune. All I ever wanted was to make my father proud." Her necklace went into the dish and she picked up her hairbrush, waving it wildly as she railed, "He wanted a son and I couldn't turn into one, but I gave him a boy and all he said was, 'Give me another one.' I had a right to tell him to go to hell, Sandro. Why can't you see that? Why can't you let me be angry?"

Her arm shot straight in punctuation and the hairbrush slid out of her grip. It skittered across the bedroom floor, landing near her shoes.

His mouth tightened as he stared at it. With a jerky nod, he said, "*Si*. He is insufferable. You were right to tell him you won't see him again." He pulled his tie loose and unbuttoned his collar, something flashing in his eyes that was both keen and sharp. Dangerous. "Come here, then."

She stayed where she was, suddenly wary. "Why?"

"I'm not going to have you tossing lamps and smashing mirrors, *cara*. If you're angry, come here. Take it out on me."

She choked out a laugh. "What do you mean? Hit you? No!"

"Do whatever you need to release this energy. I'll make sure you don't damage anything."

"Because you don't want me acting like your mother, screaming and yelling, calling him to swear and hanging up?"

"*Precisamente.*"

"You just have to control everything, don't you?" She was annoyed now, on top of her anger. "I want to *yell*, Sandro. I want to…" She lifted helpless hands and shook her fists in fury. She hadn't been this pent up and determined to let go since boarding school.

"I can see that." He finished opening his buttons and dragged his shirttails from his pants. "Come here."

There was a note in his voice on top of the command, one that said he was anticipating sex. It affected her, always, but fueled her fire tonight. She was *so* angry. Angry at her father, but angry at Sandro. At that unwavering control of his. She wanted to batter against it, break it down and break through to the man behind the armor.

Did *nothing* affect him?

Picking up the emerald drape of her skirt because it was too long now that she was out of her shoes, she swept toward him, ignoring self-preservation instincts and heading for the heart of the battle.

He opened his belt, pulled it free and dropped it away, gaze never leaving hers.

He was so tall. She wished she wore her shoes. She wanted to… Oh, he frustrated her. Reaching out, she splayed her hands on his bare waist, felt his muscles tense under her touch and dug in her nails, dragging her claws over his skin.

He bit out a curse cut by a sharp laugh, gaze flashing as he caught her wrists and pinned them behind her back, mashing her against him so she could barely move.

"You're not going to let me explode, after all?" she asked, shaking back her hair.

"Explode," he invited. "I'm here to absorb it."

She wriggled, testing his grip.

He smiled, not even exerting himself a little bit as he easily restrained her. He was that much stronger than she was. It was maddening, but inflaming, too, making her that much more determined to get a reaction from him. A strong one.

She narrowed her eyes and, quick as a cat, nipped his chest with her teeth.

"Oh, you think?" He manacled her wrists in one hand and used his free one to take a handful of her hair, dragging her head back. Rather than kiss her, though, he set his teeth against her neck, not hurting, just letting her know he could return her injury and then some if he wanted to. He had all the power here.

She struggled with more determination, but only wound up rubbing herself where he was hardening. Her breasts began to ache from the friction against his hard chest. The strap of her gown fell off her shoulder and he opened his mouth on her bared skin.

How could this be turning her on?

"This is kinky," she accused. She might have lived a sheltered life, but she read. She surfed. She knew a little about the games couples played. "Don't we need a safe word if you're going to overpower me?"

"Or you could just tell me to let you go," he said with a silent laugh, releasing her hair to push the other strap of her gown down, baring the cup of her bra. He didn't lift his gaze from the poke of her nipple against the blue lace. "Are you going to?" His voice was gruff and hungry.

When he looked at her like that, as if he was going to eat her alive, she didn't want him to ever let her go.

She struggled again, more earnest this time, seeing if he would release her. Seeing if he really could withstand this energy inside her.

He barely seemed to notice how hard she was trying, just pinned her hips to the hard length of his erection and circled her nipple with the tip of his finger.

"What if I scream?" she threatened breathlessly, wanting to.

His gaze dragged upward and his eyes were green with lust. "Do you want to be faceup or facedown on the mattress?" He began backing her toward the bed.

Her stomach flip-flopped with wicked excitement.

"You wouldn't!" She secretly loved it when they were on their knees and he was behind her. It felt earthy and animalistic and was always intensely satisfying. "Brute."

"I'm not going to hurt you, *cara*. Never," he promised as he unzipped her gown. He finally released her so he could push the dress all the way off.

She grasped at his arms so she wouldn't fall onto the bed, but he pressed her there anyway, coming down over her and covering her with his big body, thigh moving imperiously between her bare ones to part her legs wide.

She punished him by taking fistfuls of his hair and trying to drag his mouth to hers.

He allowed it as he arranged her legs around his waist, settling there as though he owned the space then returned her forceful kiss with an intrusive sweep of his tongue and a rock of his mouth that took control of hers.

Everything about what he was doing, the way he was overwhelming her but giving her this outlet for the fury inside her, excited her. She'd spent the bulk of her life seeking approval and for once she was casting away any desire for it. Something in her was pushing forth from its shell, saying *This is who I am*.

And Sandro wasn't backing off. She made noises of frustration, fought for dominance even though she was beneath him, squeezed her legs on his waist and pulled his hair. She scraped her teeth on his lips and he only lifted his head and laughed.

"You are wild tonight," he said with lusty appreciation

and peeled her hands from his hair to pin them over her head. Then he shifted so he could touch between her legs. "You've soaked them." He moved the strip of silk aside and traced her wet center, not quite giving her what she needed.

"I want you inside me," she demanded in a voice both raspy and direct. Commanding in a way she'd never been.

"The condoms are all the way over there, *cara*." He dipped one finger, letting her clasp him, which was only a tease, making her whimper. "But if you ask me nicely, I'll lick you."

"You're being a bastard," she told him.

"Close enough." He grasped her panties at her hip, giving them a yank to snap them, then released her hands and slid down the bed.

She didn't fight. In fact she groaned in abandonment as he pleasured her. It had been too long since he'd done this and he was very, very good at it. Inhibition disappeared as she said things and he did things and the energy building in her coiled to unbearable tightness. With her heels in his back and her hand in his hair, she let go with a scream that she muted with her wrist, completely lost to the moment.

She came back to a state of lassitude that was buttery and sweet.

He dragged himself to his feet and stood to strip, gaze raking her sprawling body. She was nude but for the bra that was askew across her chest. His expression tightened to stark possession and inexorable intent. He reached into the drawer of the night table without looking away from her.

She teased him, crooking her knee, letting her fingertips run up the inside of her thigh to where he couldn't seem to remove his attention.

And there, for just a second, she saw his composure

start to fracture. A shudder ran through him and he dropped the condom.

"Roll over," he ordered.

"Make me," she invited.

His stomach muscles tightened as though she'd punched him. He flared his nostrils and did it, upper lip shiny with sweat, hands shaking as he rolled her over and arranged her on her knees before he scooped up the condom and knelt behind her, one hand staying heavy on her lower back as if he wanted to be sure she would stay there.

It was a power position for him, but she felt as if she held a lot of it as he knelt behind her, gripped her hips and entered her. She groaned unreservedly and held nothing back as she relinquished herself to their raw lovemaking.

It was glorious and it affected him.

She heard it in his voice and felt it in his grip on her hips, hearing it in his curse as he fought his release. He was trying to wait for her, but it was a struggle and she loved it. She met the buck of his hips and said, "Don't stop. Keep going. It's so good, so good."

"Now," he growled, reaching to stroke and incite her. "Come with me. *Now*."

His release arrived a panting breath before hers in a guttural, almost defeated cry and a rush of heat that was as heart-poundingly satisfying as the orgasm that rocked through her like a blast wave.

As he folded over her and crushed her into the mattress, she smiled.

CHAPTER TEN

THE LIMO DROPPED them in front of the grand entrance to a mansion on the outskirts of Valencia, Spain—just about the last place Alessandro had ever wanted to show his face.

As their host and hostess greeted them, Bree was directed to take Lorenzo to an upper floor on the condition, Sorcha said, that they take the correct baby with them when they left. She wore a shimmery green gown that set off her blond hair and smiled with as much joy as Octavia did.

Sandro found a pained smile of his own. It went unseen as Sorcha hugged his wife as though they were reunited twins, leaving him to introduce himself to Cesar. It was a thankfully brief handshake since guests were arriving in a steady stream. They were invited to move inside and partake of the food, dancing and the silent auction tent.

Sandro let Octavia lead, since this was her idea, and wondered again why he had agreed to come here.

Well, he knew why he had agreed. She had come into his office a week ago, set her hip on his desk, let the slit in her wrap skirt fall open and batted her lashes.

He had leaned back in his chair, far too experienced with women to fall for any sort of sexual manipulation, not that he said so, but he had admired the effort. He was partial to those thighs of hers and when she adjusted the fall of floral fabric so he could see her hip was bare of underthings, she'd had his full attention.

"I don't ask for things very often, do I?" she'd said.

"You asked me to get up with Lorenzo this morning," he'd countered.

"I said it was your turn. That's different." Gone was the mousy wife of his first year of marriage. Octavia was much more sure of herself now, not just in her sexuality—which she used unreservedly by leaning on one arm and offering him a delicious view down her top—but in ways that kept him on his toes. She voiced her opinions and woe betide the man who questioned her judgment where her son was concerned.

He would never have expected to like having a spitfire for a wife, but it was nice to be able to let loose with some of his own forceful personality without fearing he'd flatten her.

Case in point, he took his fill of the swells of her breasts, then dragged his gaze upward without making any effort to hide his instant, rapacious desire. "Are you asking me to make love to you? I have rather a lot of work today, but for you, I can spare the time." He tossed his pen onto the desktop beside her hip.

She set the heel of her shoe, a sexy, strappy red one, on the arm of his chair, parting her legs slightly as she did. Her tongue wet her lips as though she was deciding whether to butter him up with sex first, or get his agreement before she gave him access to the sensual banquet she presented.

Either way he was enjoying the show so he was more than happy to be patient while she made up her mind. He toyed with the strap of her shoe, seeing if he could hurry the process along.

"I want to take Lorenzo to Spain," she finally said.

"Alone?" His hand instinctively closed around her narrow ankle.

"I'd prefer it if you came with us."

And he had thought, *Well played*, knowing he was done for, but he'd forced her to work for it. The shoes had stayed on and they'd brushed his ears a few minutes later. He would never again sit down at his desk without thinking of their erotic hour upon it.

But he hadn't wanted to come here. Not really. *"Sorcha needs moral support. It's her first formal party,"* Octavia had explained when they were straightening their clothes.

Alessandro looked around. The event was as polished and successful as any he'd seen. The house and grounds were ideal, the necessary elements of band and bar in place. Octavia led them out to a tent that held the silent auction items Sorcha had solicited to raise money for the excellent cause that Octavia had mentioned and now slipped his mind.

Sandro was always willing to write a check for sick children or cardiac wings, but he hated like hell to face down his own failure. He and Octavia had managed to distance themselves from the conflict of London and Primo and the baby swap. They were in a good place. His desire to revisit reminders of it was well below zero.

But he had agreed to accompany her and she, well, she'd been glowing like Christmas was coming ever since.

And her wedding rings were back in place.

Watching her as they moved through the gardens after the auction tent, he admired the way the pinprick lights in the trees made her hair and gown and eyes sparkle. The light breeze pressed the silk of her amethyst skirt against her thighs and he liked the look of it, but when she shivered in the salt-scented breeze, it was a good excuse to tuck her closer to his side.

He couldn't regret being here when he was so intensely proud to be with her no matter where they were. Pausing, he turned her, thinking a kiss in the moonlight was in order.

"Octavia," Sorcha called, interrupting. She crossed toward them with her husband. "Let's sneak away for five minutes to check the boys."

Octavia nodded enthusiastically, then glanced up at him. "Do you want to come?"

She looked very sincere, which almost made him laugh. "I have three sisters, *cara*. I know what girl talk is and when I'm likely to be in the way of it." He kissed her temple and let her go.

Then turned to face his host, a man of his own height who wore his tuxedo and old-world surroundings as comfortably as Sandro did. He suspected that, if things had been different, he might have liked Cesar Montero.

"Thank you for coming," Cesar said and canted his head toward the tent where Sandro had left a number of exorbitant bids. "And for your generosity. My wife invited you because she was anxious to see Octavia, not so we'd break records for our fundraising."

"Penance," Sandro dismissed with a shrug, accepting a glass of sangria from a passing waiter.

"Penance?" Cesar repeated with a frown. His face cleared as understanding dawned. "For the mix-up at the hospital? It was your cousin who caused it. I've read the full report from the hospital and police."

"I still feel I owe you an apology," Sandro said, hiding his discomfort behind a flat smile. "I'm very sorry your wife and son were affected."

"I wouldn't know I had a son if it hadn't happened," Cesar said bluntly. "Don't apologize. I'm grateful."

It was straight talk without sentimentality, exactly the

kind that appealed most to Sandro. He nodded, trying to take in that his habit of self-blame wasn't required here.

"The ladies have plans to lounge by the pool tomorrow, but I'll be spending the morning in our vineyard. I understand you have a private label, as well? Would you like to join me? Our head vintner would love to pick your brain on your methods."

Sandro had planned to work out of their hotel room, but it was the weekend and he found himself agreeing.

An educational morning—Cesar was a chemist with an experimental nature—was followed by a lazy few hours beside the pool, sampling from Cesar's cellar. The infants had splashed and gummed whichever finger was offered and slept side by side on a blanket in the shade. It was relaxing and very pleasant.

Later, they brought Lorenzo back to the hotel for siesta, and, once the nannies came back from their day of shopping, the Monteros would be joining them for a late dinner.

"You're spoiling me," Octavia said as she shrugged into her dress, having just fed Lorenzo and tucked him in. The sea-foam-green of her dress was paler than Sandro would have chosen for her, but the silvery shimmer made her fresh tan glow. The flouncy skirt was cute as hell, too, showing off her toned legs.

He realized she was looking at him as she put earrings in her ears, waiting for him to respond.

Spoiled? He was the one who'd just woken from an afternoon delight that had knocked him out cold.

"Why do you say that?" he asked.

"You didn't want to come to Spain at all, but you invited them for dinner."

"I drank half his cellar," he retorted. It wasn't true. They hadn't finished any bottles, but Cesar had generously opened several. "That man knows what he's doing."

Not just in the vineyard either. As Sandro had suspected, Cesar was the sort of savvy businessman he most enjoyed working with. They'd already touched on several areas with potential for partnerships. He looked forward to exploring opportunities with him.

"Well, I'm glad you're over your reservations about talking to them. I told you Sorcha didn't blame us."

"He said he wouldn't have known about his son if the baby swap hadn't happened. That he was grateful, if you can believe it. I thought I'd be squirming, but I enjoyed myself today. And since we came all this way so you could spend time with Sorcha, I thought we should do that. But I didn't expect anything good to come out of such an aggressive act," he admitted.

She stepped into tall sandals and straightened, much closer to eye level now and rather solemn.

"You and I are better because of it," she said. "If I hadn't been pushed so far by Primo and everything that happened, I don't know if I ever would have stood up for myself. I wouldn't be as happy as I am now if I still felt like you held all the power in our relationship."

"Are you happy, *cara*?" He tucked the fall of her hair behind her ear, subtly holding his breath as he waited for her to answer.

She took her time, thoughtful for a moment before allowing, "I'm happier than I've ever been." There was no subterfuge in her expression. The windows to her soul were completely unguarded, open, letting him see to the dark, reverberant, vulnerable depths inside her.

She had a way of looking at him sometimes. It wasn't hero worship. He'd seen that along with avarice and possessiveness in other women's faces. Octavia was good at disguising her feelings, but had never been motivated by anything so base. But sometimes, when she met his gaze like this, with her expression so defenseless, he had the strangest feeling she was asking something from him.

He understood now that she wanted a better life with him than she'd had as a child. He fiercely wanted to live up to whatever it was she was seeking. He'd thought he'd managed to at different times, giving her what he thought she wanted: marriage, orgasms, a baby. Spain to see her friend. Not spoiling, but meeting her needs.

At this moment, however, he wasn't so sure she wanted any of those things. What she wanted, he suspected, was love.

His heart stuttered.

He had deliberately chosen an arranged marriage to keep their hearts out of traffic. Surely this, what they had, was the perfect balance of friendship and respect, loyalty and regard, physical gratification and warm affection and the shared adoration of their son?

Her lashes swept down, hiding her eyes, but her mouth seemed to soften with disillusion. "We should go down."

"Yes," he agreed, and enjoyed touching her as they walked to the elevator. He felt pride when men turned their heads to covet his beautiful wife as they moved through the restaurant and admired her beauty himself when she smiled brightly at Sorcha and Cesar as they arrived. He even felt a measure of relief, suspecting they'd nearly detonated a land mine of some kind upstairs, but managed to step over it.

But deep, deep down, as they bantered with the other couple, touched knees, stole from each other's plates and finished each other's sentences, he felt as though they were acting. He felt like a coward.

Time marched on and Spain became a dreamy weekend Octavia hoped to repeat soon while consistently turning from that disturbing moment at the hotel, when Sandro had asked her whether she was happy. She had chosen to be honest and in being honest, she'd realize how far short from happy she really was.

Which was stupid. Her life was incredibly blessed. Ermanno was sweet and encouraging. They laughed regularly as he gradually transferred running the estate onto her shoulders. She loved this new responsibility! She'd never found a career that appealed, but every day on the estate was different yet comfortingly routine, giving her a sense of purpose and the satisfaction of contributing to things that impacted her and her family directly.

Around her, the flowers were blooming and the weather was fine. Her son was healthy and more adorable every day. He was even sleeping better and sitting up, almost six months old already. Ysabelle flew in for the occasion, bringing her count and a suitcase of gifts for Octavia along with her usual dose of exuberant energy.

She had insisted a half year birthday party was required for her grandson and summoned Sandro's sisters. They'd arrived with their children last night, surrounding Octavia in a warm, noisy way that she was beginning to cherish.

Octavia had even invited her mother and Trista had agreed to come. She'd been a different woman since Octavia had cut ties with her father, most notably because Octavia had offered her baby bonus to her mother to buy herself an apartment and she'd accepted.

As much as Octavia was enjoying a new and warmer relationship with her mother, however, she kept wondering if she'd somehow wind up just like her after all. Their circumstances were different. Their husbands were different and Octavia had told herself from the very beginning that her *marriage* would be different.

But lack of love was lack of love.

And she kept thinking of something her mother had said when they were signing the final papers for the apartment. *"He wasn't always so bitter, you know. The first miscarriages were hard on him and I think he forced himself to stop caring after that."*

Octavia wasn't in a mood to forgive her father, or even try to understand. She definitely didn't want to compare Sandro to him.

But she couldn't help thinking that if her parents had married for love rather than progeny, their relationship wouldn't have been so empty when the babies failed to arrive.

Once that hard fact had occurred to Octavia, she hadn't been able to shake it. She and Sandro had married to make a life together and they had a good one, so it wasn't fair of her to change the rules midstream and expect love.

But she did. Because she loved him.

It wasn't the nascent, immature infatuation of their first weeks of marriage, either. It was admiration for the man he was, joy at being near him, lust for his body and love, love, love of the rest of him. The emotion filled her up to overflowing, seeking expression.

She'd been working up the courage to tell him, but what she really needed courage for was hearing—maybe seeing—that he didn't love her back.

Time, she kept telling herself. He would come to love her *in time*.

Meanwhile, she would enjoy the growing love that his family seemed to reciprocate. The day was glorious so she asked for the lunch to be served alfresco. Her mother wasn't here yet, but Octavia had just finished feeding Lorenzo and left him with Bree to dress for his big day. She broke into Sandro's Fortress of Maternal Avoidance and said, "We're all on the front terrace. Will you come join us?"

He kept typing then moved the mouse, clicked and sat back in his chair. "Did I hear correctly that she's ordered a cake? He doesn't eat real food yet."

"Oh, Sandro," she said with exasperation, closing the door so his mother wouldn't overhear, then marched forward to the front of his desk. "Yes, she's gone over the top. But it's a nice day. Come enjoy it with your family."

"Ah, yes, my family. How's Papa? Got himself covered up after doing the deed with my mother in the garden this morning?" he asked with false pleasantry.

"Don't you dare embarrass her by telling her you saw them." She pointed her finger at him so he would know she was serious.

"I'm trying to forget that I did. I want to gouge out my eyes."

She rolled her own, trying not to fall into another fit of giggles at the way he'd reacted this morning. He'd been holding Lorenzo as he'd glanced out to greet the day and had abruptly let loose a string of very blue language. He'd turned away so appalled she was still snickering.

Now she tucked her chin and said, "She's happy. Isn't that the most important thing? Would you rather she was unhappy?"

"No," he said, disgruntled.

"Just not *that* happy? Are you jealous?" she asked as it occurred to her.

"What do you mean?" His gaze cut up to hers in a way that made her think she was on to something.

"Because she's with someone besides your father."

"No," he denied firmly, shrugging that off with a re-arrangement of things on his desk. "She began auditioning replacements about three months after he was in the ground. I got over that distress very quickly." He sounded as though he was telling the truth, but...

"Did you?" she pressed.

"I honestly don't care who she sleeps with." He stood, signaling that he would prefer to put an end to this conversation. His gaze came up, flat and hard. "I just didn't like watching her throw herself into relationship after relationship only to come away with a broken heart."

"I don't think he plans to break her heart. He seems as madly in love as she is." If anyone was jealous, it was Octavia. The way the count gazed at Ysabelle as if she was made of sunsets and jewels and exotic foods made her yearn to see the same undisguised feelings in her own husband's face. They had come so far, but she was greedy. She wanted more.

She wanted the dream.

Patience, she reminded herself.

"Loving someone madly is exactly what leads to broken hearts," Sandro muttered. "It's like watching a pair of trains headed for a collision that can't be avoided."

She stilled as a suspicion struck *her* like a freight engine: that she would *never* see undisguised love on her husband's face. She knew him better now, understood his aversion to deep emotion and it hit her that he wouldn't welcome the vulnerability of love. He had wanted an arranged marriage to avoid the emotional pitfalls of a love match.

Had that been one of the reasons he had chosen her? Because he knew he'd never really love her?

The heart that had been creeping onto her sleeve was suddenly yanked from the washer still damp, shaken and strung up on the line. She loved him. Irrevocably. While he, she suspected, would never, ever let himself love her back.

"Do you honestly feel like that?" she asked numbly,

not wanting to hear it, but knowing she had to face it if it was the truth.

He started to say something then paused, seeming to read something in her face that sobered him. His tongue touched his bottom lip and tension gathered around his eyes. As the silence lengthened, the significance of the moment grew.

"You do," she said, and her heart began to tremble and crack. "We'll never have that. Will we? What your mother has. Because you don't want it."

If there was a man with a stronger willpower than Sandro, she hadn't met him.

Despair crashed into her heart like his runaway train, spreading pain outward. She couldn't breathe. Couldn't do this again. When she'd had hope, it had been different, but she couldn't offer love again and know without doubt it would forever go unrequited.

"Cara," he began in that oh-so-careful tone that meant he wanted to let her down easy. "You don't want it, either. You see her happy now and think it's worth it, but when you feel that much joy, you feel the loss of it that much more cruelly. I'm protecting you. What if something happens? I wouldn't want to leave you in the sort of pain she's known."

Octavia was in pain all right. She looked away, sucking in a tight breath that burned her lungs. "I don't know why I thought— No, I do know why I thought you might come to love me. Because you're capable of it. I've seen it. You love your son and your grandfather and even your mother, despite the fact she drives you crazy. So I thought you might come to love me, but you don't. Do you?"

"Octavia." He reached across, but she backed up.

"No." She shook her head in denial. "Sex isn't enough. I told you that before we came home from London."

"You also told me you didn't expect love," he reminded grimly.

"It doesn't mean I don't want it! *No*," she said, holding him off with an upraised hand as he came around the desk. "You don't get to kiss me into thinking we're okay. I'm not okay, Sandro. My marriage was supposed to be better than my mother's. Why do you want yours to be worse?"

"We *are* better, *cara*. You know that. We're solid. Unshakeable."

"No, we're stationary. That's what I'm realizing right now. Are you really going to stand there and tell me to be happy because you're willing to love everyone around you *except* me?"

"*Cara*, you know I care about you very deeply." Pressure was drawing a white line around his mouth. "Do I really need to make love to you in the garden to prove how much? Be sensible."

"Don't mock her for loving so freely," she shot back, lips quivering and throat aching. "You told me you were coming back to this marriage wholeheartedly and you're not. You lied to me."

He flinched, head going back as if she'd slapped him.

Beyond the door, Lorenzo began to cry.

Octavia cast her husband one last baleful look and walked out the door. But it wasn't enough. As she gathered Lorenzo close and his warm, tiny body failed to drag the pieces of her heart back together, she knew she couldn't sit on the terrace and be the only person there whom Sandro would never love.

CHAPTER ELEVEN

SANDRO STOOD ROOTED to the floor, eyes closed in a wince, trying to take back the past five minutes.

And go back to what? Pretending this was never going to happen?

It wasn't supposed to! From his earliest forays into relationships, he'd known he didn't want to fall in love. All his affairs had been lighthearted and his goal for marriage had been to find a compatible partner he could respect without putting his heart on the roller coaster his mother had endured.

Octavia had been perfect. She'd come from the right background, had an honestly earned fortune and a conciliatory nature that hadn't provoked strong feelings in him.

Except in bed.

And then out of it.

Yes, he couldn't deny that his feelings for her had been growing from those first weeks of his marriage. He'd tried to stay them, had left her in London and convinced himself he hadn't missed her, but since Lorenzo's birth he'd been unable to effectively keep himself from growing more and more attached.

The attraction was never supposed to have deepened like this. Why should it have when he'd chosen her for logical reasons and they really didn't have that much in common? It was a one in a million shot that she would turn out to capture his interest so thoroughly.

But her quiet, thoughtful nature had revealed itself to also be vulnerable, then sassy. She was complex, far more intriguing than he'd first suspected. Smart and funny and loving. That was the part that had really gotten to him. She loved their son, loved his family—hell, she loved her friend from the hospital and her friend's baby.

She loved *him*.

That was the problem with emotions. With a curse, he slapped his hand on his desk so his palm stung. *Why* couldn't he control this? Why couldn't *she*? This wasn't supposed to happen. They were entering territory where real hurt could happen. Couldn't she see that?

Of course she had. When she had walked out, her last look had pulled his flesh from his bones before throwing his skin away. He'd been right back in London, seeing whatever she had felt for him shredded to nothing.

They were already in the danger zone. Hell, if he had been serious about protecting her heart, he should have left her in London when she had asked. He shouldn't have pressed and cajoled and seduced her into coming back here with him.

He shouldn't have made her fall in love with him.

Which was what he'd done. Not consciously. He'd told himself he wanted her trust. Her body. Her affection and acceptance of him.

But it was her heart he'd been courting. He wanted her *love*, damn it!

Because he loved her so much it was unbearable to think of being the only one this deeply invested.

He clenched his fists, trying to contain the massive rush of feeling as he admitted what he'd been denying. Love, thick and hot as lava seared his arteries, wrenching his heart. Who wanted this much need and anguish and possessiveness welling inside them?

Who wanted the power to hurt another and feel as though you'd punched a hole in your own chest when you did? Who wanted to be driven to open a door and go in search of a woman before he even knew what he wanted to say?

He took the back stairs because they were closer, checking Lorenzo's room and finding it empty. He tried their new bedrooms in the renovated master suite. It had a long private balcony that wrapped the corner of the topmost floor of the *castello*, offering nearly a full 360-degree view of the Ferrante lands.

It also looked onto the front terrace where his family was congregating. Octavia wasn't there, but another level below it, in the courtyard where the fountain burbled in front of the stairs at the entrance to the house, his wife was about to put his son's car seat into the backseat of her mother's car.

His heart dropped into the center of the earth.

"Octavia!" he bellowed.

She jerked and swiveled, hugging the car seat to her chest protectively. Her chin came up, up, up as she found him at the top of the house in some kind of reverse Romeo and Juliet satire.

"What the *hell* do you think you're doing?" He was shouting far louder than he had to, but all he could think was that there were too many flights of stairs between them for him to reach her before she got away. His voice had to pin her exactly where she was.

Immediately below him, his family looked up. His sister, standing near the rail, glanced down to the drive, saw Octavia and turned back to the rest of them. Her mouth and eyes formed a round O.

* * *

Octavia was aware of faces appearing across the lower terrace, but the Roman god standing at the top of the house catching thunderbolts and threatening to hurl them at her held most of her attention.

"I'm going to my mother's. I need time to think," she said. And, because Lorenzo was getting heavy, she set his car seat on the backseat inside the open door of the car.

"Do not—" Sandro roared, "—put that baby in that car."

Her mother's driver took a long, deliberate step back. Inside the car, her mother said, "Octavia, I don't like this."

On the terrace, Ysabelle's count looked up at his step-son-to-be and said, "Sandro, you need to take control of yourself."

His mother put her hand on the count's sleeve, face turned up to her son, and said, "No, *bello*. We're going to let this happen. It's been a long time coming."

For some reason, that made hope squeeze Octavia so tightly she ached. Part of her was terrified—not because her husband looked as though he was on the last peg of his control, but because she was afraid he wasn't. She was afraid he was merely upset about her taking Lorenzo, that it had nothing to do with her.

So she did the unthinkable. She goaded him.

"Fine!" she shouted, picking up the car seat and moving it to the bottom of the front steps where she set Lorenzo safely in the shade. "That's all you ever wanted from me anyway. Keep your son, then. But I'm leaving!"

She pivoted and marched to the car, throat so tight she couldn't breathe. This was too big a gamble. What if he let her go? She forced herself to turn at the open door of the car to shoot him a last, defiant look. To see what he thought of her threat.

He was no longer standing on the balcony. He'd climbed over the rail and was dangling from the bottom of it.

She clapped her hand over the squeak that left her mouth, terrified as he dropped onto the upper terrace with a thump.

"Nonna just rolled over in her grave. She hated when you did things like that," Sandro's sister told him as he straightened.

He ignored her, parting the crowd with nothing more than his unwavering sense of purpose as he headed for the rail overlooking the lawn. He vaulted as casually as he'd dropped from the top balcony, landing on the grass in a low, agile crouch.

Octavia's heart finally started again. She sucked in a stunned breath, gaze fixed on him to be sure he was okay.

He straightened to his full height and gave his shirt a nonchalant pull across his shoulders then tugged each cuff, gaze flashing silvery and livid. "Now. Explain to me again what the hell you think you're doing."

She had wanted to unleash the beast. Here he was, control shattered to reveal the dangerous inner animal that operated on pure instinct. Hunter, warrior, slayer. He was terrifying in his magnificence.

She did the only thing anyone could do when faced with such an untamed force. She turned and ran like hell.

Except she was wearing terrible shoes and his long strides crunched louder and faster behind her making her scream even before his arm snagged her. She started to buckle, but he caught her and the world spun. She wound up over his shoulder like a sack of flour as he strode back to the house.

She screamed again, kicking this time, and punched at his backside. "Put me down!"

"No."

She gripped around his waist so she wouldn't bounce and opened her mouth against his back.

"Bite me, *cara*, and I will bite you right back," he warned.

"You're making a fool of yourself!" she cried.

"I'm making a fool of both of us. Someone bring Lorenzo inside. Look after him while I deal with my wife," he said as they approached the front steps.

"Sandro, her surgery," Octavia's mother reminded in a surprisingly strong assertion, standing outside her car, purse gripped anxiously in her white hands.

He swore and paused on the stairs. The world spun again as he swung Octavia into the cradle of his arms. "Did I hurt you?" he asked with real concern.

"No. *Yes*," she corrected, so devastated by his rejection of her heart, she could barely look at him, but she did. She let him see how he'd stripped her down to a naked bud then crushed her under his heel. She wanted his love so badly. How dare he withhold it from her?

His expression twisted with remorse.

Above them, Ysabelle said dreamily, "I remember the first time his father carried me kicking and screaming into the house. Sandro was born nine months later."

Sandro bit out a curse and hefted Octavia higher against his chest as he climbed the rest of the way up the stairs and jiggled the door open.

He carried her over the threshold.

She caught her breath, sentimental enough to be ridiculously delighted by the action. Her eyes blurred with tears and the interior was dark after the brightness of the day. She could barely see, but he didn't hesitate as he crossed the foyer. He held her tighter as he took the stairs two at a time and didn't stop until they were in their room. There he kicked the door shut and crossed to set her on the bed.

She scrambled up and off it just as quickly as he dumped her there. He moved to close the balcony doors, but kept an eye on her. There was no way she'd make it to the hall door before he would be on her again.

Part of her was tempted to make that happen. It would turn into sex. In this moment, feeling as upside down as she did emotionally, turning this into a sexual battle seemed like the safer bet. Words might be hard. They might hurt. Sex would feel good, if empty.

She lowered her gaze and pressed her knuckles to her quivering lips.

Sandro's feet came into her line of vision.

"Guilt is not fun, *cara*," he said heavily. "I hate being fallible and I am. I'm human. I try to forgive myself for being a child, for having to learn the hard way the consequences of my actions, but I still blame myself for my father's death. If he had lived, my mother never would have had to scrape herself up so badly falling in and out of love with other men. I blame myself for that, too."

"It's her choice," she mumbled. "She's happy. Maybe she doesn't care if it hurts along the way."

"Maybe she doesn't, but I do. I've never wanted to go through that same sort of wringer and I'm built to. I have that temperament and I knew if I ever loved and lost, I would be just like her—completely broken. Who would ever want to feel like that?"

She turned her face to the side, struggling to hold back her flinch and the tears that flooded up into her eyes. *I'm broken*, she wanted to cry.

"I just find it really hard, Sandro." Her throat was so tight she could barely force her reedy voice to work. "Because I'm willing to take that risk. I love you. A lot. And I don't think I can bear it if you're never going to love me."

He touched her chin, gently drawing her to look at him.

"I do love you, *cara*. I knew I was in trouble the night we met, when I danced with you. I felt the chemistry and thought for a moment that the safer choice for *me* would be to let you marry Primo." His mouth twisted, but his gaze never wavered. "I wasn't about to let you go to anyone, however. And that scared me."

She swallowed, lower lip trembling against the pad of his thumb as he caressed it.

"Our honeymoon was…" His face spasmed with a hint of pain. "You call it an affair and it was, for you. I think I knew that. You were infatuated. No, listen," he hurried, not letting her interrupt. "I know what a sexual crush looks like. I've been producing them in women from an early age and yes, I did everything in my power to provoke one in you to ensure you married me, but the way I felt for you was becoming…too much. London served a lot of purposes for me," he admitted with a humble look.

She pulled in her bottom lip and sucked the salty tang of his thumbprint off it, one foot falling back so he had to let his hand drop away.

"There was a part of me that needed to prove I could get by without you, that I wasn't completely over my head," he continued, voice raw enough to lift the hairs on her arms. "Then, after everything with Primo and the birth, I knew even what little you had felt toward me was gone. Do you think I felt good after that?" His regret was palpable, making her throat ache. "No, I felt guilty and hellish and I knew I should let you go, but I couldn't bring myself to do it. I wasn't ready to admit to myself why."

His eyes were dark gray, like heavy English rain, his brow furrowed, the lines at the edges of his mouth deep.

"Especially because you weren't being open with me," he added. "You held a lot back, too."

She realized that her fingers hurt because she had them

clenched together. She searched his expression, stunned to think that she might have been hurting him with her restraint all that time when she'd only been trying to deal with her own pain.

"I've never really talked about myself," she excused. "I thought you'd be bored or annoyed, think I was complaining about nothing."

She still felt as though her inner struggles were insignificant, but glancing up, she saw she had his full attention. She swallowed, shaken.

"When I said I didn't expect you to love me, it was because I didn't think there was any reason you should," she admitted.

He cupped the side of her face. His expression was filled with adoration. "I don't understand how someone who thinks as deeply as you do doesn't see her inner value." His thumb brushed her cheek. "When you started showing your true self, I was so proud and excited and scared that I would crush you before you were out of your shell... I like this woman you're becoming, Octavia. I *love* her. In fact, that silly little word doesn't even come close to describing the vastness of what I feel." He stepped closer and framed her face with both hands, possessive. The way he looked at her was not soft and tender like Ysabelle's count, but fierce and enthralled and ravenous. "I didn't want the pain of loving, but—" He swallowed, his emotions so close to the surface his eyes gleamed. "I couldn't stop myself from falling for you."

Her mouth trembled and she wanted to duck her head, but made herself hold his gaze and allow him to see all the hesitations and insecurity and joy and gratitude and love revolving inside her like the colors in a kaleidoscope. Loving wasn't easy. It was scary and big and cost a piece of the soul. Maybe if she'd really known how powerful and potentially painful it could be, she would have fought it the way he had.

But this, when the man she loved looked back at her with the same open, vulnerable, proud and loving gaze that filled every last shadow of her being with light and warmth…it was worth it.

"I'm sorry I said I'd leave you. I didn't mean it," she said.

"Did you see the Neanderthal who came after you? I won't let you," he said with a rueful twitch at the corner of his mouth.

She smiled shakily and clasped her fingers around his wrists. "I think there's something wrong with me because I kind of liked you going caveman like that. I needed to know you would."

"Don't encourage me. I'm never proud of losing control, even if it served a higher purpose."

"Does that mean you don't want to take the makeup sex onto the balcony so they can hear us?" she asked with mock innocence, shuffling closer and lifting her lips in offering to his.

"*Cara*, we're barely going to make it to the bed."

EPILOGUE

"I'VE BEEN ALL over the house looking for you," Sandro said.

His sexy voice dragged her mind from what she held in her hand and sent a pleasurable shiver down her spine.

"I wasn't hiding," she protested with a smile, turning to meet him halfway across the nursery without dropping what she held. They embraced and kissed. It was a nice surprise to have him search her out. She didn't hesitate to interrupt him in his office if she needed him during the day, but he was usually there for most of it, running into the city once or twice a week. "What did you need?"

"Nothing. Just I saw Lorenzo outside with Bree, showing off his steps to Nonno. I decided to take a break and visit with them, but I wasn't out there very long when it occurred to me, if they were all busy out there…" His hands shifted from warm greeting to something more suggestive, straying very low on her back. "We might get busy in here."

She gave a soft, throaty laugh, leaning her hips into his as she angled back to give him a knowing look. "I'm already busy. I'm going through Lorenzo's clothes, pulling what he's grown out of."

"Bree can do that, can't she?"

Three guesses what he'd rather she did with her time right now.

"I wanted to do it." But it could wait. Sorting the piles of tiny pants and shirts made her realize how quickly their son was growing. It was exciting to see him change and develop, but made her wistful for the baby he'd been. "Look what I found."

She showed him the tag she held. It read Kelly—Boy but had Lorenzo's weight and time and date of birth. Remembering that difficult time made her heart pang, but she softened, too. If that hadn't happened, would Primo still be here, between them? Would they be like this, completely open to each other? She didn't think so.

"We've come a long way since then," he said soberly. A shadow crossed his expression, but a warm light dispelled it as he met her eyes. "Fond as I am of Enrique, I'm glad I didn't lose my son. Or you. I love you very much, you know."

"I do." She offered a tremulous smile, lifting her free hand to the side of his face. The depth and breadth of his love amazed her daily. And despite being passionate people, they seldom argued. If they happened to disagree, they were both so shocked at not being in complete accord, they each took a step back, wanting to understand the other's view immediately. Things always seemed to work out quickly from there. If that meant a lack of makeup sex, well, they had enough of every other kind they didn't miss it.

"I didn't know I could have this much love in my life," she told him. "I didn't know I could feel this much for you and Lorenzo. It makes me feel greedy for thinking…"

He lifted his brows in inquiry.

The clothes she had pulled weren't going to the charity bin. They were going into storage. She and Sandro had vaguely talked a while ago of his working out of the London office when she got pregnant again, so he could stay with her while the clinic monitored her, but that had been as far as they'd gone with their plans. Today, however, realizing how her son was leaving babyhood and becoming a toddler, she was feeling ready to expand their little family.

"I was thinking it's time to try for another," she said shyly.

"Another baby?" He caught her up in a surge of his big body, carrying her a few steps to brace her back against the wall, legs around his waist.

"No, another misprinted tag," she teased, smoothing her hand down to his shirt pocket, finding the hard shape of his phone against the flexed muscles of his pec. "Let me call Sorcha, see if she's up to meeting us in London in nine months."

"You think you're funny," he told her, forehead against hers so they were eye to eye.

"*You* think I'm funny," she told him.

"You're a little bit funny," he allowed, kissing her lightly, eyelids coming down in a smoky look of growing arousal. "Are we really going to conceive our second child in the nursery of our first?"

"That depends. Did you lock the door?"

He drew back to give her an arrogant quirk of his brow.

"Silly me. Show some faith, right?" She did have faith in him. She trusted him with her heart and her children and her life. "I love you, *caro*," she told him, squeezing her arms around his neck, heart so full tears came into her eyes.

"I love you, too, *bella*. So much the words aren't enough." He carried her to the daybed and his weight came over her as he pressed her onto it.

She sighed with pleasure, absently releasing the tag

she held as they got down to the serious business of making a new baby.

The following year, they looked at a tag that read, Ferrante—Girl. It was affixed to their newborn under Sandro's proud gaze and went unquestioned.

* * * * *

Don't miss the second story in Dani Collins's
fabulous new duet THE WRONG HEIRS
THE CONSEQUENCE HE MUST CLAIM
Out February 2016

MILLS & BOON®

MODERN™

POWER, PASSION AND IRRESISTIBLE TEMPTATION

A sneak peek at next month's titles...

In stores from 14th January 2016:

- **Leonetti's Housekeeper Bride** – Lynne Graham
- **Castelli's Virgin Widow** – Caitlin Crews
- **Helios Crowns His Mistress** – Michelle Smart
- **The Sheikh's Pregnant Prisoner** – Tara Pammi

In stores from 28th January 2016:

- **The Surprise De Angelis Baby** – Cathy Williams
- **The Consequence He Must Claim** – Dani Collins
- **Illicit Night with the Greek** – Susanna Carr
- **A Deal Sealed by Passion** – Louise Fuller

Available at WHSmith, Tesco, Asda, Eason, Amazon and Apple

Just can't wait?
Buy our books online a month before they hit the shops!
visit www.millsandboon.co.uk

These books are also available in eBook format!

6/01

MILLS & BOON®

Man of the Year

Our winning cover star will be revealed next month!

**Don't miss out on your copy
– order from millsandboon.co.uk**

Read more about Man of the Year 2016 at

www.millsandboon.co.uk/moty2016

**Have you been following our
Man of the Year 2016 campaign?**
🐦 #MOTY2016

MILLS & BOON®

Want to get more from Mills & Boon?

Here's what's available to you if you join the exclusive **Mills & Boon eBook Club** today:

✦ *Convenience – choose your books each month*

✦ *Exclusive – receive your books a month before anywhere else*

✦ *Flexibility – change your subscription at any time*

✦ *Variety – gain access to eBook-only series*

✦ *Value – subscriptions from just £3.99 a month*

So visit **www.millsandboon.co.uk/esubs** today to be a part of this exclusive eBook Club!